THE KNIGHT

SKYE WARREN

"It was not the thorn bending to the honeysuckles, but the honeysuckles embracing the thorn."

– Emily Brontë, Wuthering Heights

CHAPTER ONE

AT ONE IN the morning I wake to the sounds of a headboard banging on the wall, vibrations shooting through the hard-edged coils cradling me. It's my first night at the Rose and Crown Motel in west-side Tanglewood. Moans echo around me like the thin walls are surround-sound speakers, the man's grunts a bass undercurrent. I curl the thin blanket tight over my shoulder, eyes wide in the dark room.

At three in the morning squeals startle me awake, heart pounding, sweat slick over my skin. I push the blanket down and sit up. The rhythmic movement of the bed feels almost like a violation, as if my neighbors are touching me.

I'm not sure when I fall asleep, but when I wake up next, I'm curled sideways on the white sheet, arms tucked over my face. The red-numbered alarm clock says it's been forty-five minutes.

"Yeah…yeah…yeah, baby, like that."

He's more talkative now. And he has a slight accent I don't remember from before.

Because it's not the same man. Realization washes over me, along with humiliation for being so naive. The woman next door isn't having sex with her husband on some low-budget road trip through Tanglewood's inner city. She's a prostitute. And these men are her customers.

"You do that so good, baby. Don't stop."

I give up on sleep, because the situation hits a little close to home.

A chair and table in pale blonde wood sit beneath the air vent. Cool air brushes over my skin, bringing with it the scent of smoke and a tang I can't place. On the square table sits all my worldly possessions—the drawstring bag I used for laundry in my dorm, stuffed with as many clothes as I could carry that night. Books on ancient mythology from the semester I dropped out. There's no point in keeping them, but I couldn't bring myself to leave them behind.

A small pile of money. Not enough for my father's medicine, not nearly enough to save our house. But it will pay for this motel room for a few weeks. Food, too, if I'm careful.

"Now turn around," the man next door says, voice uneven. "I want to see that nice big ass I'm paying for. Yeah. Yeah, that's it. I fuckin' love it."

Shivers run over my skin that have nothing to do with the air vent above me. I think about the woman he's with, my faceless neighbor. What's she thinking right now? What's she feeling? Shame. Guilt. Relief. Or maybe she's smart enough to numb herself with alcohol, not feeling anything at all.

In some ways it's been easy to focus on survival since I lost my house. Where to sleep, what to eat. How to wash my clothes in the laundromat, with sticky quarters and little packets of powder from the vending machine. Easy, because survival is something I might actually accomplish. And I've failed so much. My father. And worse than that, my mother. Myself.

"Don't fight me. I want to get in that ass. It's too fucking tight. I need it."

My cheeks burn with embarrassment. *God.*

Is she scared? Resigned? Does she know I can hear them? Does she care?

I can't listen to any more.

The surfaces in the bathroom glisten with something that isn't cleaning chemicals. There's black residue climbing out of the cracks, as if the place is drawn with thick markers. It's disgusting, but at least I can turn on the water. The spray hits the scraped ceramic tub with a satisfying thud, almost drowning out the sound of sex next door. Still wearing my cami and shorts for sleep, I curl up on the lid of the toilet, knees tucked underneath my chin, a faint mist from the shower coating my face.

In the steady fall of water it isn't my neighbor's debasement I hear. It's mine.

CHAPTER TWO

ONCE UPON A time I lived in a castle. I would have defended it with my life. That wasn't what Gabriel Miller wanted from me. He wanted my innocence.

I gave it to him, but it wasn't enough.

Now I'm determined to get back my family's home.

Sunlight enters the motel room through a vertical slat between heavy curtains, splitting the room into two halves. An unmade bed on one side, a nightstand with a dusty Bible. The table and chair on the other side, with the haphazard pile of clothes and books, artifacts from a former life. A rectangle of light hits the mirror, and I use the reflection to brush my teeth and comb my hair into something half-respectable. Where I'm going there are tailored suits and high-end manicures. I've got a Smith University T-shirt and my favorite pair of jeans, thin armor in the fight of my life.

I shove all my cash into my back pocket, wrapped around my room key, unwilling to leave it behind for even a few hours. I doubt there's daily housekeeping at the Rose and Crown, and if there were, they might not steal, but I can't take any chances. My worldview has narrowed from tuition payments and charity auctions to the price of a hot dog at the corner store.

Opening the door, bright light blinds me.

I stumble over a large warm body blocking my path.

"Oh my God," I say, startled, my hands on the coarse asphalt. "I'm so sorry."

Only in the seconds following do I realize how strange it is for a man to be lying outside my door. Two decades of society manners have taught me to apologize first, ask questions later. The large figure lumbers to his feet, and I take a step back, eyes widening.

I get the impression of pale bristle and dark blue eyes. He's wearing too many layers to get a clear read on his figure, but he's tall and wide. A threat, in other words. I need to stop apologizing and start protecting myself.

"I don't have any money," I lie, half prepared to take off running. My door is still open, blocked by his body, but I'll abandon my clothes and books if I have to.

He frowns at me, a merging of bushy brows. "Don't want your fuckin' money."

It's something of a relief to realize he isn't the talkative customer from last night, but for all I know he could be one of the other men. Or he could be someone who didn't have enough money, someone who wants to take what he can't pay for.

I move back another step. "I don't want any trouble."

Though really, who wants trouble?

The man seems to grow larger without moving, a subtle shake of his large frame. I have the impression of a dog facing an encroacher, the fur on his back raised in threat. "Did I fuckin' touch you?"

The words are both an appeasement and a threat, pointing out that he hasn't hurt me even while growling the words. He may not have hurt me, but he's a strong man in a scary parking lot with a lone girl. The threat doesn't need to be spoken to be real.

"No," I say, drawing strength from somewhere inside. "But you're blocking the path to my room."

He looks back through the open door, taking

inventory of the unmade bed, the piled table. What does he see? Something to take? A dark place he can hurt me? His examination is too thorough to be completely harmless. And when he looks back at me, his eyes are shrewd. "How much?"

Shame rises like acid in my throat. He thinks I'm like the girl next door, the one with a new customer every hour. "More than you can afford," I say, which would feel better if it weren't true.

His laugh sounds rusty but authentic, as if it took him by surprise. "I bet you're fuckin' right."

He takes a step sideways with an elaborate sweep of his arm, a mocking invitation to shut my door.

It feels like a trap. Isn't this something a predator would do? As soon as I'm close to the door, he'll push me inside. He'll force me to do things, and after the soundtrack to last night, I know no one would help me if I scream.

But when you're down to two pairs of jeans, losing one is a big deal. I take a step closer, eyeing him the way I'd watch a snake on a hiking trail. There's a hard edge in his eyes, like he's seen death. Like he expects to see it again. I'm leaning away from him as I approach my door, ready to fight if he comes at me.

Instead he watches me, arms folded over his massive chest. It's not an attack, but he's not leaving me in peace either. His gaze feels intent, more serious than the wandering interest of a random homeless person.

I manage to shut the door. The heavy lock clicks into place.

This time when I look at him, it's with wry gratitude. I still don't trust the man, but there's an intimacy to his intrusion to my morning peace, a coded message in the way he stands and watches.

"What's your name?" I ask.

His eyes narrow as if he's suspicious of me. Which is funny, considering. "What's it to you?"

It shouldn't matter. "I'm Avery," I offer anyway.

His silence answers me, cold and unapologetic. I have a fortress I need to storm, so I start walking away.

"Will," he says behind me.

I pause only a moment, a hesitation in my step. A soft acknowledgment of a gift rarely given. I wouldn't call Will a friend, but I need every ally I can get. In this city I already have too many enemies.

CHAPTER THREE

THE UNEVEN SIDEWALKS lead me to the bus stop. The city's metro hisses and jolts its way through downtown until I arrive at the iron gates of a stately nursing home.

Inside, the floors are white marble with flecks of some silvery substance, glittering beneath the thrall of chandeliers. It's a luxurious space, far greater than anything I can afford.

"He had some agitation last night," the nurse says, voice soft with sympathy. "The doctor gave him medication to help him sleep. He's liable to be groggy if he wakes up soon."

"That's okay." I force a smile. "I'll just sit with him."

The truth is that he hasn't woken up in the three days since his heart attack. Not when I've been visiting him. I'm ashamed that it's been a relief. At least asleep, I know he's resting, peaceful in the knowledge that our house still belongs to me. The knowledge that his daughter hasn't auctioned her virginity. What will I tell him once he's fully conscious?

How will I explain this?

The room is dimly lit by sconces, yellow light making wood-paneled walls glow. The bed is larger than a regular hospital bed, with heavy-duty plastic rails. An antique-styled cabinet hides most of the equipment that beeps and whirs, keeping my father comfortable.

"Hi, Daddy."

He looks infinitely old against the white sheets, the skin of his hand paper-thin, inlaid with purple veins. The scars left from his attack stand out in bright relief. The sight sends a shiver through me. The enemies who attacked him are still out there. The man sneaking around the yard when we were alone in the house, too.

Some days I feel paranoid, as if our fall from grace changed me, made me a darker person. But when I look at my father, frail and broken, I know my fear is justified. Someone out there wanted him hurt. Maybe dead. Will they try again?

Not while he's here. The security at this place is as good as the food and the accommodations. The very best. The book I left here still sits on the nightstand. *Dangerous Women throughout History.* A textbook too old and worn to have much resale value. That was my excuse for keeping it, anyway. Or maybe I needed this reminder that women had been powerful despite systems designed to stop them, that we aren't always pawns in the games of men.

I sit on the edge of the bed and read aloud.

"'The face that launched a thousand ships has inspired just as many stories of what exactly happened between Helen and Paris, and how it drove Troy to war. Was it her beauty that drove men to madness? Was she a figurehead for a war rooted in economic disparity? Or is there more to her story, something beneath the surface?'"

I don't know whether he can hear me, but it's worth it to try.

And reading about Helen of Troy always brings me closer to my mother. My father used to call her that and the name fits. A beautiful woman, wife of a king. She didn't start a war—at least not that I know of. But she's the mysterious figure in my past, an enigma I can only puzzle together from stories my father told me, the same way that Helen must be sketched from countless interpretations and mentions in historical canon.

"'Helen's position in history poses deeper questions. How does she represent the ideal of beauty? And to what degree does female agency direct the course of history?'"

A murmur comes from the bed, and I glance up. Daddy's eyes are still closed, but there's a crease between his brows. I touch his hand and find it freezing. Squeezing gently, I put my other hand on his forehead.

"Daddy?"

No answer.

I swallow past the lump in my throat. "You're probably bored. I can just imagine you smiling at me, telling me that I need to stop reading where it's dark, that I'll ruin my eyes that way."

More indistinct sounds, an agitated mutter. His lips move briefly and then fall still. Is he trying to talk to me? Is he awake or dreaming?

"Can you hear me, Daddy? I'm right here."

"Helen," he says, voice rough and thin.

"That's right," I whisper, tears stinging my eyes. But I know from the tone that he hasn't heard me. At least not with any conscious thought. He's not awake, but filtering through some medicinal haze. And the yearning in his voice isn't meant for a historical figure. It's for my mother. Helen James.

"Ms. James," a voice from behind me, and I whirl with a gasp.

Past and present collide for one breathless

second, before I can right myself. It takes a second for the world to come into focus, for me to recognize the administrator for the nursing home.

"Mr. Stewart," I say, still emotional. "It's good to see you."

His expression is grave. "I'm sorry that your father's condition isn't better, but the doctor is optimistic about him. Despite his age and his injuries, his vitals are strong."

I close my eyes briefly, torn between a prayer of thanks and a plea for the future. "Thank you."

"Of course he will be at an increased risk of another heart attack, or even a stroke, with his current situation. There's a new drug on the market, an advanced antiplatelet, that can help him. The doctor can explain more details."

A new drug? That sounds expensive. And we don't have insurance.

My heart squeezes. "Of course, but I—I can't—"

The understanding in his eyes twists the knife. "You don't need to worry about that, Ms. James."

"But I—well, yes I do. You see, right now—"

"Mr. Miller has taken care of the matter."

I know that Gabriel is paying for my father's care here, but what if he stops? I don't have access to the money from the auction yet, still in trust before the thirty days end. My father could be out on the street. In his condition it would be a death sentence.

Mr. Stewart steps closer, putting his hand on mine where it rests on the arm of the chair. "Please, let me put your mind at ease. Mr. Miller has made a generous donation to our foundation. The only stipulation is that your father will have our support for as long as he needs it. So, you see, there's no reason for you to worry about that. Only focus on your father's health."

I stare at him, uncomprehending. The cost of living here is astronomical. I checked out every home in the city when my father was attacked, when he became bedridden. At the time I couldn't afford even the shoddiest bed, much less a place like this. And Gabriel Miller had paid even more than that, so much that my father was secure here for the rest of his life.

Mr. Stewart gives me a quizzical smile. "You look almost more worried, dear."

Words expand in my throat, too thick to be spoken. Confusion. Gratitude. Dread. I despise that last one, but I can't help wondering what will be required in return.

"Mr. Miller isn't family," I manage.

He isn't even a friend. No, he's an enemy.

The man who broke my father, who turned information over to the prosecutor in retaliation for stealing from him. The man who purchased my virginity in a calloused transaction. Why would he help us? He wouldn't. Which means he's only biding his time. Keeping my father alive so that he can hurt him again. Keeping me close so that he can ruin me again.

"I see," Mr. Stewart says, and I can tell that he does. Someone who's around this much family money must see some cruel things, even when they're disguised as kindness. He nods toward the book in my hands. "I heard you just now, reading to your father. That's lovely."

I shake my head. "I don't think he can hear me."

"Perhaps not, but kindness isn't only for the recipient. Sometimes it's for the giver."

"Are you saying that Gabriel Miller needed to do something kind? Why? Because he caused my father's downfall?"

A small smile. "Perhaps. But I was more interested in the subject matter. You wield more power than you think, Ms. James."

CHAPTER FOUR

I N GREEK MYTHOLOGY Helen of Troy was the
most beautiful woman in the world. There are
countless depictions of her in medieval and
Renaissance art, each according to the artist's own
interpretation of beauty. Maybe every little girl
thinks her mother is the most beautiful, but I
have no problem imagining my mother in a
flowing gown, looking out over a glittering green
sea.

That's my Helen James, a woman with multiple men vying for her hand in marriage. A woman
who married a king. A woman completely unlike
me.

So far I've dropped out of college, lost the
family home, and sold my virginity. Not exactly
anything I want told in myths years from now.

And whatever else Gabriel Miller might be,
he's not royalty.

Even so I can't deny the grandeur of the glinting building slicing through the sun. In the lobby

of Miller Industries, chandeliers made of a thousand shards shine light on a carved statue of Atlas. The earth is made of some kind of metal, its curved surface corrosive and yet somehow beautiful.

"Mr. Miller is not available," the receptionist says, eyes a pretty blank blue behind steel-rimmed spectacles.

"I know," I say, apologetic. "And I know this is unusual. But he knows who I am, I swear. We have a...personal connection. If you could just call up to him—"

She flicks a few keystrokes on her keyboard, managing to do her job while being a brick wall. "I'm sorry, but that's not possible. Mr. Miller is—"

"Not available," I finish, because she's said it a half-dozen times already.

She's determined to send me away, and I'm just as determined to stay. Whether or not Gabriel Miller intended to be kind with the donation to the nursing home, he still owns my family home. I have a slip of paper from the city proving that much.

"You can speak with the business manager assigned to your house."

Part of me knew that Gabriel might refuse to see me, but as far as I can tell, he doesn't even know I'm here. Frustration churns in my stomach, acidic and hot. He did this on purpose, sending me away just as I found out he'd taken my family's house, making sure I'd have nowhere left to turn.

"All right," I say, hollowed out.

A random employee won't be able to help me. He won't know anything about the illicit auction for my virginity or Gabriel's role in my father's downfall.

Except the person who comes to greet me isn't a man. It's a woman, her navy-blue suit accentuating a narrow waist and long, dark legs. Younger than I would have expected for a person in charge of accounts this size, only a couple years older than me.

"Ms. James," she says, her voice almost sympathetic. "I'm Charlotte Thomas. Please, let me take you upstairs. We can discuss your case."

"Oh, thank you," I manage, dimly aware of her shepherding me toward the bank of gleaming elevators. I hadn't expected to be greeted so warmly by anyone here, especially not someone who has knowledge of my family's situation.

She directs me to the elevator at the end and swipes her key card to make it open. "After you."

I step into the gilded box, acutely aware of my

plain clothes. My image is reflected back at me as the doors slide shut, a scared little girl instead of the woman I wanted to become.

"Ms. Thomas—"

"Call me Charlotte, please. Ms. Thomas is my mother." She gives a delicate shudder, mischief sparkling in her twilight eyes. "A shark of a woman."

I blink, awareness seeping over me. "Wait. Nina Thomas?"

A wide grin, beautiful but somewhat reminiscent of a shark herself. "That's her."

"She was friends with my mother," I say, at once charmed. I met Nina Thomas only a few times at society events, but she'd given me a genuine hug each time and told me I looked just like Helen James. And she'd been the maid of honor at my parents' wedding.

"I know," Charlotte says, cheerful. "Mom says they were best friends. And considering she only tolerates most people, that's saying something."

It strikes me then that Charlotte works for Gabriel Miller, the man who tore down my father with ruthless calculation, the man who bought my virginity. The man who stole my mother's house. My throat tightens with grief, the strange relief that my mother's not here to see what's happened.

Dismay must show on my face, because Charlotte touches my hand. "I know your case has…special circumstances. And I'm going to do everything I can to help."

"Does that include giving my house back?"

"No, but I'll explain the process to you and walk you through it. Mr. Miller is—"

She breaks off as the elevator dings. Doors slide open to reveal a broad expanse of carpet framed by deep mahogany walls. The art consists of two large canvases on either side, white with bold slashes of color, more texture than covering, a visual gauntlet.

"Mr. Miller is…?" I prompt her.

She glances back. "He's a hard man to understand, but he's fair."

Fair. That's one word to describe the way he purchased me, the way he fucked me.

My head spins from the new surroundings, the dim lighting. I felt small in the elevator, but it's nothing compared to this hallway. I'm Alice in Wonderland, having eaten the cake that makes me small. Everything feels oversize and dark. I'm falling, falling.

In contrast Charlotte walks brusquely across the heavy pile. "Don't be afraid," she says.

Which isn't exactly comforting.

But I follow her anyway, working to keep my head held high, fighting the strange oppressive weight of all this space. We reach a wood panel with no doorknob. The faint outline of a rectangle in the wood is the only hint that there's something here. Charlotte touches the wood, which lights up in a keyboard beneath her fingertips, some kind of glowing installation. High-tech security disguised as old-money luxury. The panel swings open, revealing an even larger office.

She leads me inside, her movements full of grace.

I feel like an unsteady colt following her, newborn and naive.

There are two wide leather chairs sitting in front of a desk the size of a car. I perch on the end of one, knees pressed together, hands squeezed between them. The hard press of denim against my skin grounds me. I'm not really falling. Or if I am, I'll have to land soon.

Charlotte perches on the edge of the desk, only a few feet away. "Your house is in a kind of financial staging area, owned by a temporary holding company pending its auction to collect debts owed."

My hands wring together. "I don't understand

how the house left my trust. It wasn't owned by my father. It shouldn't have been responsible for the judgments against him."

And a dark part of me whispered that my mother had known something like this might happen, that she'd put it into my trust to protect me no matter what my father might do.

What secrets had she known?

"I'm not sure about the trust," Charlotte says, expression apologetic. "All I know is what happened after the court seizure and subsequent placement with Miller Industries."

I know my next step needs to be visiting Uncle Landon. He's been the administrator for my trust ever since my mother died. And he told me the house was safe. But the last time I saw him was at the auction, when he called me a whore. When he told me I'd disgraced my mother's memory.

Deep breath. "Is there any way to stop the auction? What if I can pay the debt owed?"

Gabriel Miller paid one million dollars for my virginity. He put the money into escrow after the auction, but I can only collect it after a month. That means in two weeks I could pay the taxes and whatever else.

"I'm afraid it's too late for that. An auction is

the only way it can leave our possession, due to the strict regulations that define our role as a holding company."

I bite my lip. "Could I bid on the house?"

"You could," she says slowly.

"How much will it go for?"

"The bidding will start at a nominal two hundred thousand dollars. How far it goes after that…" Her slender shoulder lifts. "The house is worth several million dollars on the regular market, but in an auction houses are often sold for a fraction of their worth."

A fraction, like one million dollars? Because that's all I have. "When is the auction?"

She hesitates. "That's why I've been calling you."

I couldn't afford my cell phone anymore. "Why?"

"The auction is in two days."

Definitely falling. "No. I can't have the money by then. Why is it so soon?"

"Auctions are usually conducted with reasonable speed, so the debts are paid quickly and interest doesn't grow."

"Two days!" God, the trial and judgment for my father's case took six months.

Her pretty brown eyes don't meet mine.

"Your case has been especially fast."

Heat stings my eyes, but I refuse to cry in front of her. My hands tighten into fists, fighting the wave of emotion. "Is there any way to delay the auction?"

"You could file for an extension," she says slowly. "A lawyer could help you do that. But…"

A low voice comes from behind me. "But no judge in this city will grant the motion."

I jump to my feet and turn around, facing Gabriel Miller for the first time since he took my virginity. I had been naked that night, skin pale, a streak of red on the sheet. For all that I had been vulnerable then, I'd also worn makeup. And I had known what I was there to do, what he'd paid me to do.

My jeans and Smith College T-shirt cover me now—small comfort when I feel like a child.

"You," I say, voice shaking.

"You," he repeats, his mocking tone ringing through my bones. "Who else would be in my office?"

Charlotte hops off the desk. "I'll leave you two alone. I'm sure you have plenty to discuss."

"Thank you, Ms. Thomas," Gabriel says, an undercurrent of danger threading the words.

Wide brown eyes meet mine briefly—and I'm

not sure what message she's sending. Caution? Hope? It looks like she wasn't supposed to bring me to his office. Part of me wants to thank her. The other part of me wonders if I haven't just wandered between the jaws of a lion.

Then she's gone, and it's only the two of us in the dark cavernous space.

Gabriel stands in the shadows, a tall and looming presence. I can't see his face clearly, but his presence wraps around me like a hard embrace. And his gaze—God, I feel it like lava pouring down my body. A heavy heartbeat starts up, a rhythm that he drove into me, thrust after thrust, a visceral memory I'm not sure I'll ever quite shake.

"You stole my house," I say, my voice echoing in the wide office.

He prowls closer, light stretching over his face. And I'm shocked anew at the metallic glint to his pale brown eyes, the way they seem to glow with some incipient earthly heat. "Miller Industries took possession of the house at the request of the court. Surely you don't think I'm responsible for the entire judicial system."

His dry tone makes me want to scream. Of course he orchestrated this. "I'm going to get that extension. I'll hire a lawyer—"

"And how will you pay the retainer?" he asks, all solicitousness.

We both know I can't touch the escrow account until after the auction. "You're a horrible person."

"I'm paying for your father's medical care. I would have thought you'd be grateful."

"Grateful? He only needs it because of you!"

The accusation isn't entirely fair. Gabriel set into motion my father's downfall, which resulted in a plea deal for information. The men my father ratted out retaliated by beating him almost to death. He's been bedridden ever since.

Of course Gabriel only did that because my father cheated him.

He wanders closer, examining me from the side, forcing me to turn and face him. "I meant what I said before," he says softly. "No judge would grant the motion."

"Because they're in your pocket."

A small nod of acknowledgment. "Maybe so. Or maybe your family name doesn't hold any weight in this city since he was indicted for fraud."

I absorb the blow without any outward sign. My hopes and dreams may lie in ribbons on the ridiculously thick carpet, but he'll never see me flinch. "Yes, my father did those things. I didn't cheat you."

"Didn't you? I seem to recall paying for a full month of your services."

My cheeks heat. "You sent me away."

"And if I want you again?"

Too late. That's what I want to tell him, but I can't afford to lose the escrow. Not when there's a chance I can buy back my mother's house. "My mother never did anything to you."

"What does Helen James have to do with this?"

I narrow my eyes at the sound of her name on his lips. "That was my mother's house. She gave it to me. Not my father. Me. It was in my trust. And I don't know how you stole it—"

He makes a *tsk* sound. "Steal is such a strong word. Especially when you don't have any proof."

"And even if I did have proof, no one would care. Because my family is the black sheep of this entire city now. We're nothing and no one."

He takes a step closer, only one foot away. Close enough to see the striations of deep bronze in his eyes, to see the short dusting of hair on his jaw. "Oh no, Avery. You're someone. The toast of the whole fucking town. The girl who captivated Gabriel Miller with her pretty little hymen."

And then I do flinch.

It should hurt the most that he ruined my father, that he took my mother's house. But I can't deny the searing shame inside that he sent me away only minutes after taking my virginity.

Bitterness spikes my voice. "I don't have anything left to captivate you with now, do I? I have to beg at the secretary's desk like some stranger off the street. And then have her turn me away."

"And yet here you are." Silk on top of steel.

"You can't get mad at Charlotte for that."

"Still giving orders, little virgin? Is that something you're born with in the James family, or did they teach you that along with your ABCs?"

Rage tightens a knot in my stomach. "I'm not a virgin."

"No?" he asks, lifting a hand to my face.

I stand very still as he captures my chin between his thumb and forefinger, torn between wanting to wrench away and wanting him to kiss me. How can he make me feel alive when I've been sleepwalking for months, years? What sick twist of fate let the hands of this man bring me pleasure?

"You made sure of that." I mean the words to come out cold, unhurt. Instead I sound breathless and somehow inviting. The white carpet may as well be streaked with red. We're both back in his bedroom, both flushed and sated and ripped to shreds from what he's just done.

He lifts my face, almost tender. "I put my cock into your warm little hole. Pushed right through that thin hymen to do it. It felt like fucking heaven to break you open."

I'm a tuning fork in his hands, and the sound I make is pure arousal. "I despise you."

"You were so wet," he says, almost thoughtful. "But some of it was blood, wasn't it?"

"I'm going to find a way to get my house back."

He bends his head slightly, enough that our lips are an inch away, the words a tickle of breath against my lips. "I got off on the slide of your blood on my cock. I came that way, spilling salt into the fresh open wound."

There's nothing I wouldn't do to him, no line I wouldn't cross in this moment. My anger takes an unholy shape, rearing back with all the fury and fear of a wild horse ready to trample his enemy. "And God help me, I'm going to ruin you. The way you did my father. I'm going to *break* you."

He nudges my chin higher, exposing the vulnerable line of my throat. His mouth drops to the tender skin, a whisper of a kiss. "Do you want to make me bleed, little virgin?"

The violence takes me by surprise. My swing is wild, aimed straight for his face with all my strength. He catches my wrist midmotion, the abrupt stop shooting pain down my arm. We're frozen that way, him holding me, breathing each other's air.

"Don't call me that," I say between clenched teeth.

"Little virgin."

"I'm not. You saw the proof of it. You paid a million dollars for it."

"Actually," he says, voice deceptively mild. "I paid a million dollars to use you for a month. And as that month isn't over yet, I think I'd like to collect."

Shock courses through me, singeing every angry intention. "No."

"And as for your virginity, there are a hundred ways you haven't been taken. A thousand ways you haven't been fucked. A million dollars left to earn."

"That money's mine. You sent me away."

"And yet," he says, echoing his earlier words, "here you fucking are. This is what you wanted. This is what you came for. Did you really think you'd see me and walk away without my come inside you?"

My gasp sounds virginal even to myself. "Of course I did."

He uses the hold on my wrist to drag me closer, off balance, almost falling into him. His warmth surrounds me, along with a musk my body remembers. Alarm bells ring more than they did this morning. A strange man could hurt me, but Gabriel—he's worse. My own kryptonite.

"Here's the thing about fucking a virgin," he whispers, breath a caress on my temple. "You gave me your pretty little hymen, the small spill of blood. The first feel of those walls squeezing my cock. And there's no way to get it back, not ever. No matter who else you fuck. Even if you settle down with some prep-school fucker and let him climb on top of you every single night, I'll always be your first. You will *always* be my little virgin."

The show of possession does something strange to me. It should be offensive. It's *meant* to be offensive, but the humiliation turns liquid and hot inside my body. And the worst part is, I can't even deny the truth. He left an imprint inside me. I can still remember the stretch of him, the burn. The very shape of that heavy thickness I can feel against my stomach now. And anyone who comes after him, they'll never quite fill the space he carved inside of me.

"That's right," he murmurs, soothing now that I've acquiesced. "I've got you."

"No, we can't—"

He releases my wrist only to run a finger along my cheek. "So young. You look so young like this."

"It's the makeup," I say with difficulty. And the hair. And the clothes. In a thousand ways I was different before, the society princess. What am I now? Almost homeless. Definitely scared.

His eyes gentle, more brown than they've been before. "You didn't think you were getting fucked today. You got dressed and took the bus and came up the elevator having no idea."

"Don't feel sorry for me."

A slight smile. "Not enough to stop. Take off those clothes. Let's see what you look like when you're just a sweet, innocent college girl and not the toy I bought at auction."

And I find myself undoing my jeans, pushing them down my hips. I could fight him, but what's the point? He holds my future in his large, capable hands—the escrow account, my family's home. And impossibly he holds my sexual desire, a sudden fire that he lit with his words.

The sound of denim crumbling to the floor is loud in the wide-open room. Then I take off my shirt, dropping the soft fabric from my fingertips.

The Den is the old city building converted into a kind of meeting place for the rich, dangerous men of the city. Men like Gabriel Miller. That was where I went to ask for a loan. And it was where I auctioned myself instead. A woman named Candy prepared me that night, with waxing strips and lotions and powders. She dressed me in lingerie.

Now I'm standing in my plain white bra and plain white panties.

And underneath, the flaxen hair has started to grow back in my most private place.

Young, he called me. He meant to dismiss me, to demean me with those words, but that's not how he looks at me. His golden eyes give him away. Desire burns there, molten and pure. And the flames that burn between us feel hotter without powder and wax, without lace lingerie. They race over my skin, leaving goose bumps, tightening my nipples beneath the cotton fabric.

"The desk," he says, voice guttural. "Sit."

"Should I—" My finger hooks into the elastic waist of my panties, a nervous gesture. A question. And then, inexplicably, I blush. Red heat sweeps up my chest and scalds my cheeks. *Should I take this off?* A simple question considering what we've done together, what we'll do in the future. Somehow everything hinges on this one question.

His groan is pure agony. "I'm one breath away from bending you over the desk and fucking you raw. But I want to taste you first, so sit on the fucking desk. Fast. *Now.* Before I give in."

Taste me. He doesn't mean my mouth or anywhere else. He means down there. The private place that already has springy hair growing in, short but present.

The blush burns hotter. "I haven't… I mean, I'm not…"

His expression turns darker. "Let me see."

I push down the panties and step out of them. My eyes can't meet his, but I hear the catch of his breath. He steps close, his touch light on my stomach, my hip. Calloused fingers smoothing over bare skin. And then playing over the trim hair between my legs.

He groans a wordless denial. "You thought I wouldn't like this?"

Embarrassment turns into hot tears, more uncertainty than sadness. "Candy waxed me the night of the auction. She knows what men like."

"Let's get one thing straight, little virgin.

There's nothing you could do to your body that would make me turn away, definitely nothing as natural as this. I want you in every way and place and time. I want you so fucking bad I wish I could stop, because it goddamn hurts."

It's the closest this man has ever come to admitting weakness. The closest he'll ever come to admitting he cares about me. And it's enough to give me strength. I take a step back and perch on the edge of his desk, knees together, hands awkwardly stacked on my lap. I can let him have me, but I don't know enough to be seductive.

It seems to work anyway, sharpening his gaze on the line between my legs, the faint attempt at modesty. He slides his palm into the divide, making space for himself, grasping my thigh in a gentle hold. "So pretty," he says, almost to himself.

A shiver runs through me, currents of heat that center at his hand.

He pushes my legs open, exposing me to the cool office air. And then his body looms in front of me, nudging me wider, the crisp wool of his suit shocking against my bare skin. I'm naked and he's completely covered. I'm defenseless and he's made of walls.

One hand cradles my cheek, lifting me for a kiss. The other moves around me to unhook my bra. My nipples tighten against his chest, aching for his touch—his pinch. He's relentlessly gentle as he slides a hand down my neck, between my breasts—as he lays me back on the desk. Cold wood makes me gasp.

There's something dreamlike about this experience. Wasn't I going to fight him? Except his caresses on the insides of my thighs feel too good, painfully soft, and I don't want him to stop. It would be like fighting myself, and for once—for once I want to give in. No more taking care of my father, no more virgin auctions. No more desperate struggles in a war I can't win. Just his mouth on my stomach and lower, lower, lower.

Then his tongue touches my clit, and I arch off the desk with a cry.

"Gabriel!"

"Again," he mutters, lips glancing my clit. Then he scrapes my raw flesh with his teeth, and I can't help but obey, whispering his name again and again, in time with his tongue, a beat that exists in my temple, in my throat, in the hungry clench of my inner sex where I want him to be.

The stubble on his chin glances my slick skin. It's too much. Too much sensation, too much pleasure. I squirm away, but his large hands capture my legs. He presses me down against the smooth wood, merciless and intent. This is what surrender feels like, helpless and writhing, begging him to stop but hoping he won't.

He circles my clit, once. Twice. A third time, and my body tightens on the head of a pin. I exist as nothing but the nerves against his tongue, the starburst behind my eyes, the anguished sob that fills the room.

And even then, there's no peace. No rest from his mouth. No surcease from the hoarse demand he murmurs against my clit: "Again. Fucking again, little virgin. Until you're dripping down my chin."

He draws me tight again, and I explode into light and sound, into every hope I've ever had.

As I come down, the shadows of the room settle into place.

Behind him, the largest canvas is slashed not with color—but with black swaths. Angels and demons. Death and sex. A riot of emotion in an otherwise sterile room. "I'm going to get my house back," I say into the void.

Gabriel rests his cheek against the inside of my knee, expression stark. He looks tired, as if the weight is too much, as if I'm the only thing holding him up. It's the most intimate moment we've ever shared, the most honest. "No," he says softly, almost sadly. "You're not."

CHAPTER FIVE

I COMFORT MYSELF with the reminder that he didn't climax.

I left after his raw denial, shaken and hurt. He'd been hard beneath the placket of his trousers, intensely turned on, but he didn't try to stop me. And why should he? He'd proven his point. He could have me anytime he wanted. He'd paid for the right. He didn't get an orgasm, but he got everything else.

On the bus I consider where to go next. Uncle Landon's office?

I know we need to talk. He has to explain how the house left my trust, something he promised wouldn't happen. And even if we're not on good terms, I need his help to get it back.

Except I'm too vulnerable, so soon after Gabriel's lips made me come. I touch my cheeks as the bus rumbles through the city. Hot. Probably pink. Anyone who looks at me would know I'd been touched recently. Uncle Landon would know.

So when the stop comes for the motel, I pull the wire on the window.

The bus screeches to a halt.

There's a bakery in the strip mall near the stop. The smell of yeast and sugar greets me inside. The sweet chocolate treats catch my eye, but I can't afford them. Not when I need to make my money stretch.

It's a huge relief to know that my father is taken care of—and well taken care of. The facility has both state-of-the-art medical care and luxury accommodations. In other words my father's a lot better off than I am right now. I don't begrudge him that. After the painful months of trial and the horrible beating, he deserves the kind of care I could never give him, even working to feed and bathe him from morning to night. And the truth is, I *am* grateful to Gabriel Miller for that. And maybe that's the reason I gave in to him; maybe that's the excuse for why my body still hums with lingering pleasure.

I buy two sausage kolaches, cheap and filling. The paper bag warms my hands on the short walk to the Rose and Crown, my mouth watering from the smell.

A large figure looms to the side of my door.

My heart skips a beat before I recognize the man from this morning. Will. I'm not sure why that reassures me. He could be dangerous, but somehow I trust him.

He doesn't move as I approach, but I know he's aware of me. You'd have to be, to survive in this neighborhood. The fact that he's built like a professional linebacker doesn't hurt.

I stop in front of him. "Hi, Will."

A grunt.

"I'm Avery."

"I remember."

"Now I remember who you remind me of. Snuffleupagus."

There's a beat of surprise, then slow incredulity. "I remind you of an elephant?"

"I think he's a woolly mammoth. And yes."

Another pause, emotion flickering behind his mask. Annoyance. And maybe reluctant amusement. "If I had to be anyone, I'm the green fucker in the trash can."

"Oscar the Grouch, but I think you're more hairy than grouchy."

He shakes his head, disbelieving. "Well, this isn't Sesame Street. It's a long way from there, so what's a girl like you doing here?"

"A girl like me?"

41

His gaze feels clinical as he takes me in, head to toe. "A nice girl."

"Hey," I say, mildly affronted. "The other girls here are probably nice."

He snorts, looking sideways at the row of doors. "You're defending Chastity? She'd knock out your teeth just to get rid of the competition."

"You don't know that. We could be friends." But I make a mental note to err on the side of caution and avoid my neighbor. I'm pretty sure in a street fight I'd be on the losing side.

He glances at my bag, long lashes over dirt-darkened cheeks. "What you got?"

My stomach churns, scraping the sides for any trace of yesterday's meal. "Pigs in a blanket." My hand tightens on the waxy paper. "I got one for you."

Blue eyes meet mine, narrowing. "No, you didn't."

"Do you want it or not?" Without waiting for him to answer, I open the door to my room.

I push inside, holding the door open without looking. After a beat I feel his large presence behind me, the weight of the door leaving my fingertips as he comes inside. My stomach pitches with uncertainty. What if I made a mistake inviting him in? But anyone who remembers

Sesame Street can't be all bad. Gabriel would probably mock me for being that naive, but I already have a lion after me. It can't hurt to have a woolly mammoth on my side.

When he's inside I realize that there's only one chair at the small table. Will solves that problem by leaning against the wall, arms folded, chin down. I sit on the opposite side. I serve the pigs on a blanket on top of napkins from yesterday's fast-food lunch. It's a far cry from the Michelin-star restaurants my father took me to, but the spice and salt on my tongue couldn't taste better.

I swallow the first bite, savoring the hint of smoke.

When I open my eyes, I see Will down his entire kolache in a single bite. Then it's gone, and I realize how hungry he must get, how much food it must take to sustain his frame. He's not fat; in fact I suspect he's painfully lean under the layers of jackets. A man that tall and broad shouldered is meant to be hearty.

"Stop," he snaps at me.

"Stop what?"

"Looking at me with those puppy-dog eyes. I'm not going to take your food too."

I glance down at the rest of the kolache in my

hand. He could use this more than me. And I do have some money to get more. Maybe there's another way to make it stretch. Maybe—

"Christ," he says, voice tinged with frustration. "I told you this wasn't fucking Sesame Street. The people here will take as much as you give them, and then take more than that."

Anger strengthens my resolve. It's one thing to share my food, another thing to be lectured by him about it. "If that were true, you could have taken the bag when I first got here."

"Hey, just trying to help. The sooner you get out of here the better."

Lord save me from men trying to help. They're the reason I'm in this mess.

"Excuse me if my trust fund suddenly disappeared, but this is all I can afford right now." The sarcasm in my voice covers up the fact that I actually *did* have a trust fund. And it actually did suddenly disappear.

He shakes his head. "You want to end up like Chastity? Go right ahead."

Sunlight punctuates his words as he opens the door. Then he's gone, leaving me in darkness.

Chastity. I wonder if it's her real name. If so, it's a cruel irony. It might just be pretend, a stage name, meant to entice men with faux innocence.

That's what men like, isn't it? Youth and naivete. A blank slate to impress themselves upon.

I remember the men at the auction for my virginity. God, I can never forget their rabid expressions, their hungry eyes. What is it about inexperience that drives them crazy?

Why does being untouched matter so much?

I've been touched. Between my legs I can still feel the echo of Gabriel's tongue. But it's a long way from the sexual experience of Chastity. Multiple men, night after night. My stomach clenches, threatening to throw up the single bite. I close my eyes, fighting the reaction. Will may be an asshole, but he's right. The sooner I get out of here, the better.

CHAPTER SIX

THE SOUNDS OF moaning, of grunting, of cursing follow me into my dreams. They turn into demons and angels, pleasure and pain—into a man with golden-brown eyes and sharp words.

The next morning I take a little extra time doing my hair and makeup. A strong woman looks back at me, pretty and confident—like the portrait of my mother that hung over the fireplace. Except at my age she had been in college and wearing a promise ring from my father. Today I'm going to visit Uncle Landon to find out what happened to my house, on the outside looking in to my own life.

Shoving the key and cash into my back pocket, I head out the door.

And stop in my tracks.

A sleek black limo idles in the center of the parking lot, the gleaming black stark against the backdrop of cracked concrete and cigarette-littered gravel. *It's not for me,* I tell myself. It can't be.

It's probably one of Chastity's customers.

At eight o'clock in the morning. In the cheapest motel in Tanglewood.

The driver steps out and nods to me in that deferent, discreet way that drivers have. My stomach sinks. He opens the back door and stands beside it, a silent invitation. A tacit command from the man inside.

My feet move me across the pavement, breath trapped. It's that moment when you've slammed your finger in a door, before the pain has registered, when your mind is all too aware of what comes next.

The shadowed interior hides his face, but I know who it is before he speaks.

"Good morning," comes the low voice of the man who made me come on his desk. The door shuts behind me, enclosing me in the warm darkness.

"What are you doing here?"

A shuffle of papers. The scratch of a pen. As the darkness solidifies, I see him reclined in the back of the limo, focused on a stack of papers in front of him. Working, like I'm a distraction. "I'm your ride."

He doesn't even look up. "Excuse me?"

"To Landon Moore's office. That is where you're going, I assume."

My eyes narrow. "How do you know that?"

Finally he looks up, his golden gaze searing me. "Because you'll do anything to get your house back. It's the only place you feel safe, isn't it? The only place you felt loved?"

My stomach clenches. "How did you know where to find me?"

"I don't think you need me to answer that."

Because he knows everything that happens in the city. He could have had me followed after I left his office yesterday, but odds are he knew where I was before. "Thanks, but no thanks. I'd rather walk on nails than ride with you."

I pull the latch to discover that the door is locked. From the inside.

My gaze flies to him. "You're kidnapping me?"

"Unfortunately," he says with fake sympathy. "You'll have to explain to the cops how I abducted you and transported you in comfort to your previously planned destination."

The car glides forward, as if connected to his very will.

Asshole.

I glare at him, settling into the warm leather.

Are these seats heated? Of course they are. I have to admit this is way more comfortable than the city bus, but everything has a cost. And when it comes to Gabriel Miller, the cost is always too high. "Why are you doing this?"

"Does it matter?" he asks, his voice faintly mocking. "As a gentleman your comfort is my highest priority. It's enough to be of service to you."

"You're not a gentleman."

"Probably right. In that case I'm coming with you to see sweet old Uncle Landon give you the horrible news, to see your face fall as he assures you there's nothing you can do."

My throat constricts. "Can't you find someone else to torture?"

"No one nearly as pretty. Besides, my presence has some advantages."

"My very own supply of fire and brimstone?"

"People are more inclined to tell the truth when I'm in the room. My reputation for dealing with liars and cheats is somewhat brutal." He leans forward, his eyes reflecting sunlight. "All of it true, I'm afraid."

I'm living proof of that, the fallout from my father's decision to steal. "Be careful or I might think you're actually being nice to me."

A short laugh. "Not a chance. It will be my pleasure to see Landon Moore break. And even sweeter to watch you break, too. A show I can't pass up."

Any warm, fuzzy feelings evaporate. I lean back in the seat, arms crossed. "Fine."

He nods toward the sideboard, where a white paper box sits on the wood inlay. "There's breakfast if you're hungry."

I want to tell him exactly where to shove his food. Except my stomach chooses that moment to growl, squeezing as if to emphasize its emptiness. And when I peek under the flap, the steaming buttermilk waffles look too good to pass up. I'd rather believe that he's being nice with the limo ride and the food. Maybe then it would feel less like I'm being fattened up for the slaughter.

CHAPTER SEVEN

U NCLE LANDON WORKS in a row of historic houses that have been converted to exclusive office space. It takes both a large monthly fee and personal connections to score a lease here. A wooden sign nestled in a pile of heart bougainvillea proclaims the office of Landon Moore, Financial Advisor. He's been a family friend since before I was born. A trusted confidant. And the executor of my trust.

I climb the stone steps and knock on the stately door. He normally operates by appointment only, but the James family has never needed them. And he hasn't answered any of my calls from the pay phone on the corner since I got to the Rose and Crown.

Of course I dread seeing him again. The last time we met was at my virginity auction. That will be the most embarrassing part of this conversation, especially with Gabriel Miller in tow, an amused spectator. But not the most important part.

There's a sound behind the door. I imagine Uncle Landon peeking through the peephole, weighing his options. He might just ignore me, and I'll have to come back another day.

But the door opens, revealing the man who got me my first bike, the man I viewed as a family member. The man who offered to marry me because I look like my mother.

"Avery," he says, sounding tired. His face looks drawn, hair askew. "What are you doing here?"

"We need to talk. They took my house."

He waves a hand like it doesn't matter, gesturing to Gabriel behind me. "And I see he isn't letting you out of his sight. I suppose I can't blame him after the obscene amount he paid."

Then Uncle Landon doesn't know that Gabriel sent me away after taking my virginity. And I see no reason to set him straight. It's as good an excuse as any for Gabriel to be here.

I step into the living room that's been converted to a small waiting area. And realize the lights are off. The desk is empty. "Where's Patricia?"

Patricia has been his secretary for as long as I can remember. When my dad used to bring me,

I'd wait on the couch with a *Highlights* magazine. Patricia would help me with the hidden pictures.

Uncle Landon shakes his head, waving his hand again as if swatting away a fly. "She's gone. Not important."

I glance back, but Gabriel has a blank expression. When we reach Uncle Landon's office I know something is very wrong. Normally he's meticulous, every stack of paper perfectly aligned, every book in its proper shelf. But now the office is in disarray, books turned over and laddered high, a dark spill of coffee soaking into someone's tax returns.

"Uncle Landon, what's going on?"

He mutters something about housecleaning. "Wasn't expecting you."

"I've been calling you." Furtive trips to the phone booth on the corner, frantic messages into an answering machine that probably hasn't been checked. "You said the house would be safe."

He falls into his chair, looking weary and ten years older than he had at the auction, head in his hand. "I'm sorry, Helen. I know you loved the house."

Alarm strums through me. "Helen was my mother."

Cloudy eyes look through me. "I failed you,

and I'll never forgive myself for that."

"What did you do, Uncle Landon? Why did I lose the house?"

Gabriel steps from the shadows. His palm hits the square foot of exposed desk, the sound startling. "Tell her, Moore. She needs to know. I'm sure she doesn't want this public any more than you do."

Uncle Landon focuses on me, regret darkening his eyes. "I got into trouble, my girl. The market crash. Bad investments. My clients, some of them are powerful. They would have come after me if I didn't lessen the blow to their portfolios."

Dread clenches my stomach. "Is that what happened to my trust? The market crash?"

He shakes his head, silent.

Gabriel picks up a piece of paper from the desk, scanning it briefly before tossing it to the ground like trash. "Fake paper trails. Moving money around like no one would ever notice. And he almost got away with it, because there are enough naive trusting fools in the world."

I stand, shaking from within. "And I'm a fool?" I ask Uncle Landon softly.

He doesn't meet my eyes. "You weren't a fool, but you were trusting. Because your mother and your father trusted me. And you looked at me like family."

"That wasn't just my money you stole. It was theirs, what they had put aside for me." The house my father built for my mother, her pride and joy. "That house."

"I know," he says, mournful. "I tried to save it. When you authorized payments for your father's restitution, I slipped more money out. If you had married me when I asked, you never would have known. We could have sold the house."

"And lived in a marriage built on lies?" And worse, a horrible substitution—because it's really my mother he wants.

"What do you have now?" Uncle Landon demands, angry and desperate. "A million dollars! Women like you always end up on your feet, don't you?"

"Women like me?"

"Like your mother," he spits. "So beautiful. Everyone wanted her. But I was the only one who really knew her, who loved her. And she chose your father."

Jealousy fills the air, sick and scented black. "How dare you. My father trusted you."

"I know," Uncle Landon says, his voice breaking. "I know."

And to my horror and shock he breaks down into wrenching sobs.

"He was the fool," Gabriel says softly.

My laugh sounds sharp, cutting me into pieces on the way out. "Don't spare my feelings now. I know you think I'm stupid. Gullible. Blind to what's in front of me."

"Maybe. Or maybe you're loyal and optimistic."

"Either way," I say bitterly. "The result is the same. I lost the house."

"Did you?" Gabriel asks mildly.

"The auction," Uncle Landon gasps. "You can bid on the house."

Hope sinks its claws into my heart, painful and unwelcome. "I don't have the money yet. It's in escrow until the end of the month. And the auction is tomorrow."

Uncle Landon rifles through the papers on his desk. "It's still an asset, one with conditions. You can use it as a guarantee of payment as long as the bank confirms its release." He freezes without looking up. "The guarantor would have to sign as well."

The guarantor. That would be Gabriel Miller.

Now I know the real reason he came along. So

that he could tell me no. So that he could break me just one more time. I look at him, my heart already breaking.

Except he doesn't look at me with fake regret, with thinly veiled amusement. He doesn't smirk and tell me that I look so beautiful when I'm shattered.

Instead he pulls out a pen, businesslike. "It will need to be notarized."

I stare at him in disbelief. "Excuse me?"

"If you want the representative of the holding company to validate an offer, it will need to be notarized." He looks completely calm, as if he didn't just offer me hope.

"Wait," Uncle Landon says. "You need to think about this. The money in that escrow account is all you have left. If you spend all of it, even most of it, on the house, you won't have anything left. How will you pay for maintenance, taxes—"

"I'll figure it out."

Uncle Landon gives Gabriel a brooding glance. "That's how you got into this mess. You can take the money and build a new life for yourself. Get an apartment. Go back to college."

My heart squeezes with the desire to have those things back. To join Harper at the parties and late night study sessions. That world seems foreign now. Gabriel wasn't so wrong when he said it was the only place where I felt safe. The only place I felt loved.

Stay here, sweetheart. Stay small. That's when you're safe. Stay safe.

"No," I say, my voice strong. "I want the house."

"Why?" Uncle Landon shakes his head, already mourning the loss.

"Sometimes people need what they need," Gabriel says softly. "Doesn't matter what it costs. Doesn't matter what they give up to get it. It's a question of survival."

I turn back, surprised by the gravity of his tone.

Gabriel isn't looking at Uncle Landon. He's staring at me, as if his words are about my virginity instead of the house. As if I'm necessary to his survival. Except that can't be true.

Uncle Landon moves into action, appearing twenty years younger as he lunges for his phone. I only distantly hear him talking to someone, telling them to get to the office right away. Shock seems to hold my body in place, like I'm carved out of concrete at the park. And he's the sun, perpetually shining down on me, heating me from the outside in.

"You'll outbid me," I whisper, clinging to my despair.

I'm not sure I can survive a second blow.

Gabriel shakes his head slowly, gaze trained on mine. "It would be a conflict of interest for me to bid on a house managed by my own holding company. A violation of our contract with the city." His voice turns wry. "And I wouldn't want to jeopardize my standing by doing something illegal."

The bland note is a private joke between the two of us, who both know that he's done a hundred illegal things, a thousand, and would do them again. But he won't do this. That's the promise his golden eyes make in the dank office. He would hurt me, but he wouldn't lie to me. Not about this.

And that means there's a chance I can win my mother's house back.

CHAPTER EIGHT

THE NEXT TWO hours are a blur of paperwork and stifling waiting.

Soon after Uncle Landon makes the phone call, the quaint old office floods with people. A haggard-looking Patricia, her hair a dark silver instead of platinum blonde. A representative from my bank. Charlotte Thomas, from Miller Industries. I need to be prequalified to participate in bidding.

Gabriel signs his form shortly after the notary arrives. With a curt nod he takes his leave from the group. He barely glances at me before striding from the room, presumably taking the sleek limo with him. I pretend that's why I'm disappointed, that I'll have to take the bus home.

Not because I want to spend more time with him.

Except that when I step outside, the limo idles down the street.

As I watch, the driver pulls closer and then

steps out to greet me. My heart speeds up, dangerous anticipation flooding my mouth with remembered spice. Fear? Or arousal?

The limo is empty.

I scoot onto the plush leather, my chest strangely tight at the realization that he left the limo for my comfort. Warm seats embrace me as we ride through the city, leaving the upscale Old Tanglewood where Uncle Landon works and entering the seedy downtown where I've taken up residence. From behind tinted glass I see people give the limo weighted looks—covetous or wary. This must be how people look at Gabriel Miller, the man himself.

When we pull into the parking lot, the driver opens my door. "Mr. Miller asked me to tell you I'll pick you up tomorrow. The auction begins at three p.m."

"Thank you."

I watch as the limo glides away, crunching rocks as it goes. What strange gestures, both the rides and the permission to bid on the house. *Be careful or I might think you're actually being nice to me,* I told him. But I hadn't believed it. Except what other explanation is there?

Unless he's waiting to surprise me at the auction with something horrible.

I can't shake the dread as I cross the parking lot. Maybe that's because Will isn't in his usual spot by my door. Probably just out wandering. Maybe working. Worry makes my heart skip a beat. He's strong enough to defend himself, but there could be multiple men. Knives. Guns.

A thousand real incarnations for the monsters in old mythology.

And more than any childish character, he reminds me of Odysseus. Longing for home.

Resolved to watch for him tonight, I swipe the card and enter the room. Only to shriek as someone flings their arms around me. "Harper!"

She laughs, only a little apology in her expression. "Sorry! I wanted to surprise you."

My heart thuds in lingering fear. "Shit. Well, you did. What are you doing here?"

Her hip nudges mine, and I can't stay mad. "Act like you're happy to see me."

A smile breaks the gloom that settled over me after Gabriel left. "God, I am. You asshole."

"You love me. Besides, I tried calling you."

"How did you even know where I am?"

"I called the worst motels in the city and offered blowjobs for information," she says matter-of-factly.

"The worst part is that I believe you."

"I gave your landlord a bag of peanuts from the plane and a crisp Benjamin in exchange for a key. He seemed chuffed. I don't think he expected that much, really."

Based on the economics of the area I suspect he can buy more than one blowjob with a hundred dollars. Maybe from my neighbor Chastity. "You really shouldn't be here. This area has, oh, I don't know, a hundred percent crime rate. Your stepbrother would lose his shit if he found out."

"That's what I'm hoping," she says cheerfully. "Besides, you're here. How bad can it be?"

In response I double-check that the door is locked and close the extra security latch. "He really gave you a key? That's not very reassuring."

"I'd sell you out for a crisp Benjamin," she says, hopping on the bed.

I roll my eyes. "Okay, but you're not staying here. You're going to call a cab and get a room at the Ritz or something."

"Please, a cab is more dangerous than staying here. Especially in this part of town. Come on. We can order a pizza and pretend to be camping."

"I'm pretty sure you can't use a motel room for that. Or pizza delivery."

She grins. "And you can tell me ghost stories.

About the ghost of your virginity."

I make a face at her. "A lady doesn't kiss and tell."

"Fine, then you can tell me about the limo that dropped you off."

"Is there any gossip you don't know?"

"I hope not."

I settle into the chair where I shared kolaches with Will. "Did you see a guy by my door when you came in?"

"Big and shaggy, like the abominable snowman?"

"He is not," I say, affronted. "The woolly mammoth, maybe."

"Is that really less insulting?" she asks dubiously. "Yeah, the hotel guy ran him off. Said he'd call the cops. The homeless guy cussed him out but left."

Damn. "Okay."

"A new love interest?"

"Please. The word *new* implies there were any before."

"Gabriel Miller seems to be taking up a lot of your attention lately."

"He's a horrible person." I'm not so sure that's true anymore. What if letting me leave early was a kindness? What if he really is trying to help me get my mother's house back?

Her expression turns sly. "You can still want a horrible person."

I crumple up a coarse napkin and throw it at her. "I don't, okay? That's crazy."

"She doth protest," she says, throwing it back. "And anyway I didn't mean him. I meant Justin. Cute guy. Captain of the rowing team. Used to be your fiancé. Am I ringing any bells?"

"That was over the second he broke up with me."

"He doesn't think so. He's on some kind of quest to save you."

That sounds ominous. "I'm serious. We're done. I could never trust someone who left me when I needed him most. He abandoned me because my family didn't have money anymore. Because his daddy told him to. How messed up is that?"

"You don't believe in second chances?"

I need a second chance myself too much to say no. "This is a heavy conversation to have without alcohol."

She reaches into her bag and pulls out a two-liter of soda and a bottle of coconut rum. "So prepared. Now let's build a fire and roast some marshmallows. I want to hear everything."

CHAPTER NINE

I DON'T TELL her everything. Though it doesn't have to do with being a lady. I'm pretty sure I gave up any rights to the term when I sold my virginity to a room full of cigar-smoking, brandy-drinking men.

But I tell her enough to hear her opinion on the house auction.

"I think he's sincere," she decides. "He had a crisis of conscience when he fucked you, and now he's trying to make it up to you by giving you what you lost."

"My virginity?"

She giggles. "Would you want that back?"

"God no. Totally useless. The only thing that ever got me was a million dollars."

Halfway through the coconut rum, both of us find that hilarious. We drink the rest of it over a pepperoni pizza while she tells me about Justin's fall from grace. He was Tanglewood's golden boy. The son of a state senator, poised to follow in his footsteps.

And in another lifetime, my fiancé.

I'm not sure which hurt more, the fact that he broke off our engagement or that he'd done it over the phone. When he heard about the auction, when he heard about Gabriel Miller, he'd shown up at Gabriel's estate. It was some half-cocked rescue mission, his figurative armor still shiny from disuse. He decided to be my knight on a whim—and he abandoned me to my fate the same way.

"Are you sure a million dollars will be enough?" she asks.

"No, but I'm crossing my fingers. And toes. And everything."

"I'll cross mine too."

"The house is worth a lot more, but Charlotte said the auctions usually go for less than market value. I'm hoping this one will be even less than that, since it belonged to the James family. History matters for houses like this, and no one even takes our calls, much less wants our house."

"Finally, an upside to your total ruin."

"I'll drink to that."

Total ruin. If there's one thing I can say about Gabriel Miller, he's thorough. His goals aren't good, his methods rarely kind, but you can depend on his ruthlessness. In a perverse way I can count on him more than I could count on Justin.

I sleep that night with a deep, dreamless security that only alcohol can bring.

CHAPTER TEN

HORRIBLE POUNDING DRAGS me out of sleep. I squint against the harsh sunlight streaming between the vertical blinds. What's happening? It sounds like the entire motel is coming down. Construction? Asteroids? Anything seems possible in my delirious confusion. There's a warm weight across my legs, holding me down.

"Gabriel?"

The world comes into focus, and I realize it's Harper's legs pinning me down. And I said Gabriel's name. *Out loud.* How embarrassing. At least Harper is more groggy than me.

"What's happening?" she mumbles, dragging a pillow over her head.

The events from yesterday come back to me in reverse order: the late-night chat, finding Harper in my room. Meeting with Uncle Landon. Oh God. The auction. It's today!

A knock comes at the door, more insistent.

"Coming," I shout, fighting with Harper's

limbs and the sheets around my ankles.

Harper groans. "Make it stop."

I fling open the door to find Will standing outside the door. His brown eyes widen as he takes in my state of undress—a tank top and panties. A small sound of surprise and I slam the door shut. "Why are you knocking?" I call through the door. I know from Chastity's soundtrack how thin these walls are.

"There's a limo in the parking lot. Pretty sure it's for you."

"Ten minutes," I shout.

"Whatever," comes the reply.

The water here takes forever to warm up, but the upside to freezing cold water is I'm wide awake after my shower. I brush my hair and throw on jeans and a T-shirt, this one announcing my inclusion in the Prep Academy chess club. Glancing at myself in the mirror, with damp hair and no makeup, I look like I might be in high school—not about to bid a million dollars in a high-stakes fight for my family.

A knock comes again.

I fling open the door, shouting, "I said I'm coming."

The driver stands there, expression carefully blank. "Yes, of course."

"Sorry," I say, blushing. I look sideways, but Will has disappeared. "I'm ready."

"Yes, miss."

Harper seems to have gone back to sleep, judging from the soft, somehow feminine snore, so I don't bother to wake her. Instead I throw myself into the back seat of the limo, breathless and urgent. He rolls out of the parking lot with careful slowness. How late am I?

Nervously I tap on the dividing window.

It rolls down. "Yes, miss?"

"Umm, what time is it?"

"Ten o'clock."

I blink. "I thought the auction doesn't start until three."

"Mr. Miller thought you might like to spend time in the house before the auction."

Because I might not win. This might be my last chance to see my mother's home.

"Oh. That's…nice of him." Suspicion rises up, and I force it back down. Why do I always think the worst of Gabriel Miller? Oh, that's right—because he systematically destroyed my family and defiled me.

"Yes, miss."

And I have a new resource at my disposal to learn something—the driver. What kind of chess player would I be if I didn't take advantage of an opening?

"What's your name?" I ask.

"Byron," he says, sounding cautious himself.

Apparently exposure to Gabriel Miller heightens paranoia. The driver might have signed some kind of nondisclosure agreement. But I don't want to know particulars of his habits. And I definitely don't want any business secrets. What I want to know about is the man.

Purely for manipulative purposes, of course. Not because I actually care about him.

"How long have you worked for Gabriel?"

A pause. "Six years, miss."

I try to keep my voice casual, as if I'm making conversation—even if we both know I'm fishing. Can he blame me? Both he and I are pawns in Gabriel's game. Small pieces to be moved around. Unimportant. Powerless. Imagine what we could accomplish if we worked together.

"Were you a driver before that?"

"In a manner of speaking." There's another pause, longer this time. I can almost see the roadblock he's putting up in front of me, the warning signs to turn back. In the end he lets me through. "I was in prison, actually. Before that I drove for an armored car company."

Prison? My throat tightens. "Oh."

He continues with less hesitation, as if now that he's made the decision to tell me, he can share everything. "I got mixed up with a bad crew. They had this plan to knock over a bank, using the armored driver as an inside man. And I would have gone along with it, too."

Curiosity gets the best of me. "Why didn't you?"

"When we got close, the plan changed. First I was going to be the only one armed, and I wouldn't have shot anyone. But then they got ahold of some automatic weapons. They claimed they wouldn't hurt anyone, but it started getting out of hand. I didn't want to do it, but I was in too deep."

I'm leaning forward in the seat, literally on edge. "What happened?"

"It was too late to bow out. I knew too much. They would have offed me and then done it anyway. So I tipped off the cops and went in as their inside man instead."

"Oh my God."

"Never thought I'd be a rat, but I couldn't let anyone get hurt."

My breath is caught. "Did anyone get hurt?"

"Only me. When shit hit the fan, the cops

came busting in. My buddy, all the way from grade school, he saw that I'd snitched. Shot me once in the chest before they brought him down."

"Oh no."

"Had a couple surgeries. By the time I woke up, most of the plea deals had been made. I took what they gave me. Three years in minimum security for my part."

I frown. "That seems like a lot. You helped them."

"I should have locked in a plea deal before handing over the information, I guess. Should have had a better lawyer. I didn't mind too much. Minimum security isn't a bad gig."

"And Gabriel hired you when you were released?"

Another pause. "Before I was released."

Before. "What could you do from inside?"

"He had a friend in there. Three months. Make sure he makes it through and I'd have a big bonus when I got out. He gave me the bonus and offered me a job too. Said anyone strong and loyal had a place with him."

"That sounds like Gabriel."

We pull off the freeway into an area with large estates and gated communities. Affluent. Exclusive. A place I had always felt at home, but it looks foreign now. I'm a tourist in my own country.

We reach my driveway, the limo rocking over the old cobblestone. I stare out the window at the unkempt bushes, the forlorn birdbath. Everything in disrepair. "Would you say he's a good man?"

"No, miss."

"Why not?"

"Because he wouldn't like me saying so. He wants everyone to think he's dangerous and cruel. Sometimes he is. But only when he needs to be." He pulls the limo to a slow halt in the circular drive. His eyes meet mine in the rearview mirror. "I'd call him a fair man. You take care of him, he'll take care of you."

Chapter Eleven

I GREW UP in this house, stealing warm cookies from the baking sheet when Rosita made them, finding every nook and cranny to hide my dolls. And after my mother died, the house became my conduit to her. A temple with which both my father and I worshipped her memory.

Anticipation speeds my heartbeat as I cross the front walk.

The engraving on the front door looks foreign after only a few weeks away. I examine it with the kind of detachment I might use in an art gallery. Beautiful architectural detail. Nothing more.

It doesn't feel like home.

That will change once I've won the auction. It has to.

Inside the air feels different. More dusty. More dry. The rooms are mostly bare from when I sold the furniture to estate dealers and antique stores, desperate for money. Not enough. Never enough until I auctioned the most valuable piece left—myself.

Upstairs I find my bedroom the way I left it, a plain mattress on the floor. Some old posters on the wall—overly colorful kittens and the grinning face of a male pop star. The room of a teenager, never updated when I moved to college and definitely not when I came back.

It's a little like looking at a museum. A sepia photograph.

History, not the present.

That will change once I have the house back, once I can take down the posters and buy back antique furniture for the rooms. A small voice whispers, *what if it doesn't?* Except if I'm not fighting for my mother's house, I don't know what to fight for. This is all I have left.

A shiver runs through me, as if the house is haunted.

I leave the room and wander the empty hall-ways, aimless and melancholy. And it strikes me suddenly that I might be the specter haunting the house. My sudden laugh cuts off abruptly, strange in the hollow space.

At the end of the hall a small door leads to old metal stairs. I spent some time in the dusty attic when my father got sick, sifting through stacks of antique headboards and trunks of old dresses.

Some of it was sold along with the furniture in the house. Whatever's left was too broken or too personal to be of any value.

The lights don't work up here, the wiring too old and faulty. Instead I pulled down boards from the stained glass window so I could see. As soon as I open the low door, blue and yellow light floats down from the top. The smell of old paper and cedar draws me up the stairs. Stained boxes hold the only things with any meaning left in the house.

I kneel beside one and find Christmas decorations, an angel's wings chewed through by some long-dead rodent. Another box has pictures, and I smile at the sight of my father. Tears prick my eyes. I visited him in the hospital two days ago, after his heart attack. He was barely conscious, still recovering and heavily medicated, which was almost a relief.

When he wakes up, he'll have questions. I'm not sure how to tell him that I lost the house, that I auctioned my virginity to get it back.

Not sure how to tell him that it was all for nothing.

If I win the auction today, I won't have to tell him anything. He'll be able to return home, to live out his final days in the only place that reminds him of my mother.

Dust-coated brocade drapes pile on top of a box in the corner. I shove them aside, sneezing at the cloud that rises. The window shines a purple hue on stacks of yellowed paper. Invitations to coming-out balls and engagement parties. Correspondence with my father's friends from his alma mater.

From a sheath of newspaper clippings, a book slips out. A thud on the floor resounds in the musty air. I pick up the book made of old leather, soft to the touch, wrapped with a long strip of the same material. There's nothing marking the cover. I open it, revealing thin pages hand stitched. The first page has only one thing scrawled in perfect, looping penmanship: Helen Avery Lancaster. My mother's maiden name.

My knees weaken, and I sink onto the nearest closed trunk.

A turn of the page reveals more of her handwriting in straight lines across.

Since my debut is in one week, it seems fitting to begin a new journal. This is my new life as an adult, eligible to be married—and to hear Mother tell it, as quickly as possible. I understand what's at stake. Although Mother refuses to speak about such uncouth matters as money, Father isn't nearly so circumspect.

Still, I won't say yes to the first boy who offers for me.

No matter how rich he is.

A diary, from before my mother married my father. Maybe even before she met him. My heart expands, filling my chest and pressing against my ribs. I've seen a hundred pictures, spoken to her husband, her friends, but I've never heard her words. Never imagined I would get to see through her eyes.

"I thought I'd find you here."

I whirl to face Gabriel Miller, my heart beating too fast from my discovery. He's wearing an overcoat still dappled with rain, hair dampened, eyes glinting gold. I'm breathless and a little bit wary. Somehow the diary ends up tucked behind me, hiding it before I've fully decided to.

He notices, of course. Stepping over an embroidered ottoman, he crosses the slats to me. "Let's see what you've found."

The discovery feels too powerful to hold inside. I ache to share my excitement, my awe, but it's still too fresh. Too private, especially for the eyes of my sworn enemy. He waits with excruciating patience. Slowly, reluctantly, I pull the diary from behind my back. The brown leather cover doesn't reveal anything. "Nothing much. Just an old notebook."

One eyebrow rises. "Is that right? You won't mind if I look at it, then?"

Without waiting for me to answer, he plucks the diary from my hands.

"How dare you." I move to snatch it back, but he's already heading deeper into the attic, toward the stained-glass window where the light is better.

He reads from a page in the middle. "My mother insists that I accept Geoffrey's offer. The James fortune is unmatched in Tanglewood society." He pauses to glance at me. "How mercenary. I suppose it runs in the family."

Rage burns through my veins. "You don't know anything about my mother. Give that back to me. Right now."

He's too tall, holding the diary out of reach as he reads further. "She would accept Landon Moore, even though his family has fallen in society recently, but I can't. I just can't." He makes a *tsk* sound. "Poor old Uncle Landon."

My fists beat his back, fueled by righteous fury. "That's not yours."

"Isn't it?" He cocks his head to the side, considering. "I own the holding company. And the holding company owns the house and everything inside."

I grow still. "You're going to keep it?"

"What a dilemma," he says with faux sympathy, turning back to the page, reading again. "And the man I truly want has no money, no family name. No chance of winning my father's approval. We both know that it's impossible, but the heart doesn't believe in boundaries."

My heartbeat pounds in my ears. My righteous indignation toward Gabriel is eclipsed by the realization that my mother loved another man. At least she did once.

I know from archeological mythology that history isn't about facts—it's a story told by the survivors. The victors, both literal and figurative. I know that she married Geoffrey James, my father. They were wed until her death. Theirs was a happy marriage, a loving one, or so I thought. What if there's another side to the story? Hers.

"Give me that."

He slaps the diary shut, examining the well-worn cover. "No, I don't believe I will."

"It's mine."

"Actually I believe it belongs to your mother, but that's neither here nor there. The holding company couldn't possibly let go of something materially valuable to the property."

"The diary isn't going to affect the auction!"

"Won't it? I think you'll bid higher if the diary is included." He slips the diary into his inside coat pocket.

"I'm already willing to bid everything I have."

"Did you consider that I might be protecting you? You might not like what you find inside."

"No," I say, taking a step closer. We're chest to chest, face-to-face. Or we would be if I wasn't a full foot shorter than him. "Because you don't know what's in that journal, so how could you know whether I'll like it? And besides, you don't want to protect me. You want to hurt me."

He draws a finger down my cheek, almost tender. "You might be right about that. I get hard just thinking about your blood on my sheets."

My hand is up before I can consider the consequences, slapping him across the face. In the aftermath, my hand hurts more than I would have expected. And his head is turned away. From the side I can see the corner of his lips turn up.

When he faces me, there's no warmth in his golden-brown eyes. The fire has frozen, crystallized like the frosted glass that lights his face. "God, you really did forget. You thought I was your knight in fucking armor, riding in to defend your castle."

"No," I whisper, but I'm terrified he's right.

That the limo driver and Charlotte Thomas and even Harper's drunken declarations of Gabriel's regret convinced me that he's a good man. I thought I had kept my guard up, but now I see how utterly defenseless I am. He's not going to save my castle. He's going to burn it down.

Amusement would be easier to bear. The genuine sympathy lighting his eyes makes my stomach turn over. "My sweet little virgin," he murmurs. "Always thinking the best of people. Even when they don't deserve it."

A single tear escapes my lashes, rolling down my cheek. "I don't."

"Oh, but you do. Did you think I bought you out of kindness? That I couldn't bear to see you touched by any of those other men?"

"No," I whisper, broken.

"Or maybe you believed I started to care for you, that I couldn't bear to hurt you anymore."

I shake my head in wordless denial. He sees too deep into my heart, into dreams I never dared to speak. Hoping for the impossible. A lion could never fall in love with a mouse.

He steps closer, tucking a strand of hair behind my ear. "I fell madly in love with your beautiful little cunt. I loved the way it felt around my cock. I dream about it, darling."

"Go to hell."

"Maybe I should ask for your father's permission to marry your sweet pussy."

"Stop it." I'm infuriated, almost out of breath with the force of my anger.

"Mr. James, I know that you and I have many differences, but I hope we can come together over our mutual enjoyment of a good fuck."

"Don't you dare talk about him. You don't know anything about him."

"I think you're the one in the dark where your father is concerned."

A scoffing sound escapes me. "And I should believe anything you say? You already gave fake evidence to the prosecutor so that you could get your revenge. You ruined him."

"He cheated me."

"That excuse is getting old. So what? He cheated you. You have more than enough money, and he has nothing. Don't you care that he's suffering? Don't you see that he's lost everything?"

"Not his loyal daughter. You rushed to his side as soon as you left me."

"He had a heart attack!"

"And what if I'm sick," he says, mocking. "Will you rush to my bedside?"

"Yes," I say, words sharp with venom. "I'll be

there to watch your pain. And I'll enjoy it."

A chuckle. "Something to look forward to."

I stalk away, trying to clear my head. Mind games. He's only doing this to mess with me. He doesn't care about the diary—and he doesn't care about me, either. It's about winning for him.

Turning to face him, I force myself to lower my eyes, to speak in deference. "Please, Gabriel. There must be some way I can convince you to give me the diary."

His surprise ripples through the air, almost tangible. "What are you doing?"

"I thought you would like this," I say, keeping my chin lowered, my voice soft.

If he wants me to beg, I'll do it. If he needs this to feel like he won, I'll give that to him. The diary is worth everything to me. More than the house. It has the answers to my mother.

The key to unlock my family's past.

His stillness echoes louder than any command, settling around me like vines.

There's something dark about being with Gabriel here—in the house where I grew up. In the legacy he took from me. In the place he might help me get back.

My voice is low. "What do you want?"

"Everything."

"I've already given you that."

"Not even close." He stalks around me, circling like a predator. "I want you bent over and broken. I want you bleeding at my feet, little virgin."

I shiver despite my determination. "You're depraved."

"That's right." He stands behind me, large hands clasped gently on my waist. It would be a tender embrace if I didn't know his intentions. "And you're the object of my depravity, the target of every dark wish, the canvas I want to paint. I won't be satisfied until I've marked every inch of you, inside and out."

A hard swallow. "Then why did you let me go?"

"Ah, little virgin," he says gently. "So that I could chase you."

CHAPTER TWELVE

I KNEW WHERE my mother was going based on the jewels she wore. Pearls for charity luncheons. Diamonds for society balls. That night she wore a large ruby pendant, a necklace I'd never seen before.

Where are you going, Mama?

A party, she said absently.

Can I come?

Her laugh was a strange sound. *You're too young, Avery. And thank God for that.*

When will I be old enough?

She looked at me, her eyes softening. *I don't know, but it's nothing to rush. Stay here, sweetheart. Stay small. That's when you're safe. Stay safe.*

She left that night and never came home.

A drunk driver hit her. She died on the way to the hospital.

Daddy told me what happened in a rough voice, eyes red from crying. My eight-year-old brain didn't want to believe it. I searched the house for her, convinced she was playing hide-and-seek, hoping that it was all a bad dream.

When I finally accepted she was gone, I crawled into bed and stayed there for two weeks. Both Daddy and Rosita begged me to eat, but I could only curl up beneath the covers, huddled in the dark as if the cramped, airless space wasn't in the world without my mother.

As if it would keep me safe.

Gabriel reaches for me, and I react on instinct.

I whirl, dashing for the metal stairs. A low ottoman catches my foot, and I land hard on my knees. I can feel Gabriel behind me—his breath, his excitement. And then his hand on my wrist.

Something wild rattles inside me, and I let it free.

Without looking I kick backward, pulling a grunt from him. His grip loosens enough for me to twist away, and then I'm flying down the metal steps, dashing through the hallway.

I know this house better than him, but without furniture there's nowhere to hide. Instinct alone propels me down the hall, hair flying behind me, breath shallow.

On some level I know it's useless to run. He'll only enjoy it. But the deeper animal side of me recognized the danger in his eyes. The sharpness of his teeth.

I'm acting on pure survival. Fight-or-flight.

My room is an empty shell, an architectural dig into the time before.

The time when I was still innocent.

Footsteps follow me—closer, closer.

I duck into the closet and hold my breath. This is how I played hide-and-seek with my mother, shaking with nervousness as I heard her voice. *Where is my little Avery? She's quiet as a mouse!*

And then he's in my room. He stills.

"Where could you be?" comes his liquid voice. "So small. So sweet. I can almost smell you."

Because he's a wild animal made to look human. A predator living among prey.

Anxiety clenches my throat. It's a struggle not to move, but even flat against the wall my heart beats wildly. He must hear it. He must feel it vibrating through the house.

He crosses the room with a leisurely stride, hitting that board that creaks ever since I spilled a glass of water. I can envision him looking out the window at the unkempt lawn.

"The chase makes it better, don't you think? If I touched you, would you be wet?"

No. It's impossible.

Except there's heat coursing through me. Anticipation. And my body can't seem to tell the difference between fear and arousal. Or maybe they're the same thing, mixed together by the sexual awakening of the auction. Maybe I only get turned on by a man owning me.

The doorknob turns. The closet door opens, letting in a sliver of light.

He steps inside, blocking the light with his body. "Found you," he murmurs.

"You never really let me go."

A low laugh is the only response.

Because it's the truth. He toys with me, letting me run only to pick me up by my tail. It's a twisted game, meant to amuse him, meant to scare me.

Mr. Miller thought you might like to spend time in the house before the auction.

This is why he had the limo pick me up early. Not kindness. Not understanding. Pure sexual power, made colder by the fact that we're in the house he took from me.

It's already wrong to be here with him in my family's legacy. Already humiliating to be hunted like an animal. That's what he means to do— break my spirit. Twist my love.

Even knowing I'll lose, I'm not ready to give

in.

I tilt my face to his, lips inches away. He wants my capture more than my surrender, so I let him cover the distance. His lips claim mine in a bruising statement. He invades me with tongue and teeth, with force and electric pleasure—for five seconds. Four. Three, two, one.

And then I bite down, hard enough to taste the copper of his blood, brutal enough to hear him grunt in response. It's the follow-up knee between his legs that makes him stumble back. The powerful force of him thuds against the wall, and I know I only have seconds of freedom.

Then I'm flying down the stairs, through empty halls and echoing wood floors. My breath comes in rasping, frantic gulps as I burst into the large living room, the grand fireplace almost naked without my mother's portrait above it.

It's in that moment, the half heartbeat where I mourn the loss of her picture, that Gabriel slams into me from behind. Then I'm pressed against hand-carved scrolls, marble cold against my cheek, patterns sharp against my body. Without thinking my hands go to the mantel, holding me steady while he presses from behind.

He's breathing hard too, though it seems more like excitement than tiredness. Especially with the hard length imprinted against my ass. "You drew blood," he murmurs, almost with wonder.

I jerk against him, but his hold is too secure this time. "Good."

Heat. Softness. The faint edge of teeth. That's how his mouth registers against my neck. Sensation and pleasure and pain as he works his way to the curve of my shoulder.

"No one fights me like you," he says, his hand flat against my stomach.

My breath catches. It's a threat, that hand. The one safe place on the front of my body. Any higher and he'll touch my breasts. Lower and he'll reach between my legs.

"Will you fight me?" he murmurs.

It only makes him harder, hotter. It only makes the win more satisfying for him.

There are some things a body will do on its own—like taking a deep breath at the bottom of the ocean, knowing you'll only breathe in water but having to try anyway. "Yes."

"Thank fuck," he says, his voice thick.

He turns me around, his mouth fusing to mine, stealing my breath. I don't have a chance to push him away; he's already inside me. His mouth bites at mine, hard enough to make me jolt, sweet

SKYE WARREN

enough to make my nipples pebble beneath my bra.

I push up against his chest, an implacable wall as hard as the brick behind me. "Wait."

"There's no time," he breathes, his lips working down my throat. "They'll start arriving any second now."

My eyes close in tacit denial. "No."

"No?" He dips lower, into the hollow of my neck. "I wish I could taste your cunt. Wish I could lick you—here."

The nudge of his hips pushes something hot and hard against me. Between my legs. We fit together perfectly. "Not here."

"Later," he promises.

Then his mouth is on mine again, his body pressed against me—the broad plain of his chest, the bunch of his abs, the ridge where his body demands entry. So much need coiled in him, so many ways he could relieve it, but all he does is kiss me.

Maybe that's why I lean back and let him.

His hand drops lower, curving around my ass, supporting me as I press close, my body aching for a fullness only he can supply. The rhythm starts between my legs and spreads outward.

My body turns to light, bright and sharp. He's the inky black sky, holding me in place.

The slam of a car door jolts me from the reverie.

I stiffen, realizing what I let him do. And I want even more. He straightens my clothes with an efficiency I can only marvel at. I still have one foot in the other world, the one with light and color and pure sweet sensation.

His eyes are a shocking mahogany now, as if he's a stranger. He looks almost tender as he tucks a strand of hair behind my ear. "Better than I remember," he whispers.

I trace his lips with my fingertips, wondering how he can be so cruel and so kind. Does it tear him apart inside? Or does it lock into place like a perfect jigsaw puzzle, made perfect by the way it fits together?

"Mr. Miller? Are you here?" The female voice slices between us.

He takes a step back. "That's Ms. Thomas, here to inspect the home prior to the auction. I'll go out first, give you time to regain your bearings."

He's all business now, and I mourn the loss. "Are you staying for the auction?"

"I wouldn't miss it."

Because he wants to see me lose? Or because he wants me to win? The small sting of hope must be some side effect of our encounter. I feel as if I sleepwalked and woke up by the fireplace, having dreamed the entire thing. Only I'm not sure when I fell asleep—in the attic?

Or maybe I went to sleep as a child, curled up in my bed, only waking now.

CHAPTER THIRTEEN

THE LAST DAY I spent in bed after Mama died Daddy came to me, his expression dark. He studied me with a grave finality, and I felt that deep pull to please him.

The bed dipped as he sat on the side.

"Look at what she did to us, Avery. She shouldn't have gone that night. This is happening because she left."

My eyes are wide. He was sad when we got the call about Mama. Desperate when he begged me to eat. I'd never seen him angry like this. "It wasn't her fault."

His gaze lands on me, a strange intensity. "You won't leave, will you?" When I don't answer right away, he demands, "Will you?"

My tummy clenches. "I won't, Daddy."

He regards me with approval. "There's my good girl. This is where you're safe."

It seemed to be true. My childhood here was marked by kind smiles and warm parties.

That makes it all the more jarring when some of the men who arrive were at the auction for my virginity. I understand that there are only so many men in Tanglewood who have huge amounts of money to spend, but I feel paranoid too. As if they want to possess me in every way possible. There's a man with gray hair who had a beautiful woman in a glamorous dress—now the same woman has her hair in a tight bun, a suit crafted to her body.

Gabriel Miller stood at the back of the room at my auction, taunting me, challenging me, until he finally threw out the winning bid. Now he stands at the back in a different capacity, as the temporary owner of this home. Not gaining something today. Losing something.

"The opening bid will be low," Charlotte whispers, taking me aside as the attendees tour the house. "The last thing you want to do is get in a bidding war, going up in increments. That kind of thing is going to end high. These guys are competitive. They want to win."

"But they all have more money than me. They can win if they want to."

"That's why you need to go high fast. I know it's counterintuitive, but it's—"

"Game theory," I say, because sociology was a

major component of ancient mythology. In a sequential game, the more bids there are the more complex the decision tree. And in the case of an auction, the only direction to go is up. "The sooner I win the better chance I have of winning at all."

"Exactly," she says before hurrying over to a man with questions. All of them are allowed to inspect the house prior to the auction.

There are folding chairs brought in, which only emphasizes the lack of furniture. More and more the house is hollow, a once-grand oak tree now brittle and dead.

"We're about to begin," Charlotte announces.

Some men in suits sit down, holding cardboard placards. I head over to Gabriel, determined to ignore my embarrassment. The knowing glint in his eyes speaks to mouths and hands, to the touch I can still feel in the secret places on my body.

"The diary," I say, my voice soft so no one else hears.

He shakes his head slowly. "I think I'll hold on to it."

Desperation is a fist around my heart. "Please, Gabriel."

"I do love hearing you say my name. Even

more when you're naked and spread wide, when—"

"Stop." My cheeks flush. "It's my mother's diary. She means everything to me. And if I don't win this auction, it's all I'll have left."

"Then you should try to win."

Helplessness steals the air from me. I want to slap him again, but then everyone in the room would see my anger. My weakness. Most of them already know that Gabriel Miller bought me at auction. They know we've had sex, even if they don't know he was touching me just minutes ago. I won't let them see me affected by it.

I look at the fireplace, where a portrait of my mother used to hang. Even that was sold to an estate dealer, the artist famous enough to command a decent resale value. "Tell me this much. Do you think a million dollars is enough?"

With his command of real estate, with his personal knowledge of the people in this room, he will know how the bidding will be. "The truth is, I'm not sure."

Charlotte stands beside a small folding table, about to begin.

"Gabriel," I say, pleading.

One eyebrow rises. "I'm telling you what I know. It would usually be enough. The bad press about your father kept away some of the big players. Everyone here wants it for a quick flip or a conversation piece—neither is worth very much."

"So I can win?"

"If you play it right, you might. But…" He looks thoughtful.

"Last call," Charlotte says, gaze directly on me.

"But what?" I whisper.

"But the man on the end there? I don't know him."

A wild card? I look at the last row where a man in a tailored suit glances at his watch. I've never seen him before either. And Gabriel knows everyone.

Without another word I hurry back to find a seat—right up front, because I don't want to miss anything. Charlotte hands me a cardboard number and returns to the table.

I want that diary, but first I need to win the house back. This is where my father wants to spend his final days. This is the place that holds my family's legacy. My mother left it to me for a reason, and I won't let her down.

"The bidding starts at two hundred thousand," Charlotte says. "The contract will be signed on immediate conclusion of the winning bid. Anyone who hasn't already prequalified will be required to present proof of fiduciary capability. Any questions?"

"Are you free Saturday night?" a man near the front says.

Charlotte gives him a flat look. "Why? Do you know anyone worth my time?"

The men laugh, except for the man in the corner. He looks impatient. And except for Gabriel. His sharp look promises some small retribution for the disrespect, but the other men don't seem to notice. That's why he stands in the back, I realize. To watch over everyone. An almost godlike presence who metes out punishment and rewards. I've become intimately familiar with both the pain and the pleasure at his hands.

"Let's begin," Charlotte says brusquely. "Do I have two hundred thousand? Two hundred?"

It's clear that she's done this before. It's also clear the other men have plenty of experience. Their cards lift only an inch when they bid, such a tiny distance to signify thousands of dollars.

My stomach ties itself into knots and then straight again by the time the bidding lands where I need it. "Three hundred thousand," Charlotte says.

That's my cue. I raise my placard high. "One million dollars."

The room falls silent. "Can you repeat that?" Charlotte asks.

"I'll bid one million dollars for the house."

The silence stretches out for one heartbeat, two, as I wait to find out if I've won.

"Well," Charlotte says, sounding pleased. "That certainly changes the game, gentlemen. What do you think? Are you willing to put more than one million into this house?"

One of the men stands. "Too rich for my blood."

With that he's on the phone talking to a broker about a different property, already moved on before he even strides from the room.

The gray-haired man who was at my auction, who came close to bidding on me, stands as well. When he turns to me, his eyes are kind. "Congratulations, young lady. I must say that I had thought the house would be an enticement to have you after Gabriel here, but in both cases I appear to be outgunned."

With a cordial bow he leaves, his gorgeous assistant in tow.

The only man left in the audience is the one in the corner, the stranger who even Gabriel didn't know. He's been impatient this entire time, looking as if he'd rather be somewhere else, but now he leans forward. "What's the next bid?"

Charlotte pauses, hiding her dismay behind a cool smile. "One point five million, anyone?"

My throat closes. I would never be able to match that. I can't spend a dollar over a million. I know that Charlotte is trying to help me, but the dread in my bones tells me it won't work. There's some reason this man is here, some purpose I can't discern.

The stranger lifts his placard.

And just like that I lose everything.

CHAPTER FOURTEEN

T HE MOTEL ROOM is empty. Harper's Louis
Vuitton steamer bag is still on the floor,
overflowing with a sparkle dress and unicorn
socks. Worry eclipses my grief over losing the
house. What if someone else convinced the motel
owner to let them inside? There's no sign of a
struggle, except for the assortment of lotions and
bath bombs strewn over the bathroom counter.

I head outside, following the sounds of banging and drunken laughter.

Behind the motel a wall of boxes and trash
cans do little to hide a makeshift camp. I realize
this is where Will must sleep every night, in one
of the low stacks of blankets tucked against the
wall. There must be more men than I realize, but
only two figures surround the fire rising out of a
rust-coated barrel. Sitting on a crate is a hulking
figure with a low rumbling voice.

On the opposite side of the fire an animated
Harper tells a story with her hands. I don't even

have the energy to get mad at her for being reckless. It's so quintessentially Harper to make friends with anyone and everyone. And besides, the circle looks inviting to me now, when my heart feels heavy as a stone, eyes burning from the tears I shed on the way home.

Will spots me first. "You look like hell."

Harper takes one look at me and envelops me in a hug, her slender arms surprisingly strong. "Oh no," she murmurs. "That asshole. That fucker. I'll kick his ass."

I give her a watery laugh. "Thank you, but it wasn't Gabriel. At least I don't think so."

"Sit down," she says, guiding me to an up-turned blue cooler. "We have cheap beer and all night long. What the hell happened?"

"I went early, before the auction. In the attic I found a diary that belonged to my mother. I never even knew she kept one."

And the men she talked about, vying for her hand. Her reluctance to agree to my father's proposal. She should have been going to concerts with friends, thinking about a career, but Tanglewood high society had very strict rules for women.

Even twenty years later, for me, there hadn't been much give.

My throat tightens. "There's so much about her I didn't know."

"That's amazing," Harper says.

"It would be, except I don't have it." There are some things too personal to share, and what Gabriel Miller did to me against the fireplace is one of them. "The diary was part of the house, so it went to whoever won the auction."

Will makes a rough sound. "Rich people out to make a buck."

I'm not sure if he knows that Harper is richer than God—at least, when her stepbrother gives her permission to use her trust. "I don't know if it was a real estate person. Gabriel hadn't seen him before. He didn't talk to anyone else. But he seemed intent on buying the house. As if he would have spent anything."

Harper looks thoughtful. "Like he wanted to live there?"

"No, he didn't seem interested in the house itself. He kept looking at his phone, like he wanted to get out of there. It was strange."

They're silent a moment, digesting this. Then Will holds something out. It takes me a second to realize that it's a joint, rolled up thick and short. Justin did some partying with his frat brothers. I went with him when he asked, but he knew I preferred to stay in. Movie nights. Study sessions. That's more my speed. And I knew it would crush my father if I was caught with something.

I don't have to worry about his opinion now. He's not aware enough to ask questions, but I've already failed at everything. Dropped out of college, my fund depleted to pay his court-ordered restitution. Lost my mother's house. And that's nothing compared to his horror if he learned I had auctioned my virginity. I never plan to tell him the worst part, but any claim to fatherly pride is long gone.

Why shouldn't I have fun now? What else is there to lose?

I take the joint and put it to my lips. A deep breath.

And a cough. "Oh my God."

"My little innocent," Harper says, taking the joint from me. "That was your first hit, wasn't it? You took too much."

Will eyes me with suspicion, as if I just revealed that I'm armed and dangerous. "How old are you exactly? You aren't jailbait, are you?"

"Of course not," I say, grabbing a sweat-slicked can of beer from the stash. "I'm going to turn twenty-one in two weeks."

"That's not actually old enough to drink,"

Will says, not appeased.

"She's eighteen," I say, pointing at Harper. "The genius skipped a few grades."

"Tattletale," Harper says before taking a drag.

Will shakes his head. "Kids these days."

"I can't believe Gabriel didn't buy the house for you," Harper says, studying the smoke from the fire as if it contains the answers.

"He couldn't. Something about Miller Industries being the court-appointed holding company, so if he bid on the auction, it would be a conflict of interest."

She shrugs as if unimpressed. "He knows other rich people. A couple mil is nothing to them. Surely he could have gotten it if he wanted to."

"I don't see why he would. He already gave me a million dollars."

"Still think he's an asshole," Harper says, passing the joint to Will.

"I agree," Will says.

"What do you even know about it?" I say, uncomfortable with their assessment. I know that Gabriel Miller is an asshole, but somehow it feels weird for other people to point it out. I have a strange impulse to defend him that I force down.

"I know that anyone who lets you live in this

shit hole isn't a good guy," Will says.

I put my head in my hands, defeat washing over me in waves. "I can't believe I lost the house."

"It's Gabriel Miller's fault," Harper says in a pragmatic tone. "He's behind everything—your father's trials, losing the money. Even the auction for your virginity."

He's always been the man behind the curtain, making everyone dance, tearing down my family brick by brick. And I let him touch me. I almost came for him against the fireplace.

"Give me that," I say, reaching my hand out for the joint.

After a slight hesitation, Will gives it to me. "Not too much."

I take a deep drag, desperate for any oblivion I can find. After a minute the world feels a little sharper, my body alive in a new way. As if my skin can smell and see and hear the world around me. As if the air around me speaks. "Wow," I breathe.

Harper nods in satisfaction. "We'll do a ritual cleanse."

Another drag. "What?"

"My mom taught me this. In between husbands three and four she got into this pagan phase, like with divining crystals and tea leaves. Most of it's bunk, but I like the cleanses."

"Is this another one of your juice fast things? Because I don't have a juicer in my motel room. Or, you know, fruits and vegetables."

"No, silly. This is where you expel someone negative from your life."

And then I can't help myself. "I'm not sure Gabriel Miller is really negative. I mean, he is. But in his own way there's a reason for it. He hasn't hurt me specifically."

Will looks skeptical. "He's the reason you're here?"

"He doesn't have to be evil," Harper says. "Even though he kind of is. It can even be someone who's good and kind. It just means that they're negative *to you,* so this helps you remove their influence. Like imagine there's an invisible string between you and them. This is cutting the string, setting you free."

Free. That sounded good.

Because where was I, really? With a million dollars and a father in a nursing home. A sad state of affairs but not an impossible one. I could build a life this way, if I could let go of my old one. If I could forget Gabriel Miller. "How does this work, then?"

"We need some herbs to throw in the fire. Sage. Maybe rosemary." Harper bites her lip, looking all of eight years old as she struggles to remember.

Will glances around. "There might be some grass where the concrete's busted."

Harper pulls a small bundle wrapped in tissue paper from a paper bag. "This will work. It's almost like an herb."

"Is that marijuana?" I'm not sure why I'm even asking. Sage and rosemary won't make me forget about Gabriel any more than this joint has.

"It's medicinal," Will says gravely, as if we're performing a serious operation.

"Fine," I say, taking another drag. I really do need to be high for this. "But if I'm going to do this, you guys have to, too. There must be someone you should cut out of your lives."

"Christopher," Harper says immediately.

Her stepbrother has been a thorn in her side ever since her father married his mother. The fact that they since divorced made things easier, but when her father died, they found out he'd put Christopher in charge of her trust.

"The cleanse isn't supposed to have bad effects on the person, is it?" I ask, because Christopher's a good guy. In fact the only time I met him, he was both nice and funny. Except whenever he has to deal with Harper, he seems to turn into the Grinch. They're a bad match, but I wouldn't want him harmed—even by a pretend ritual cleanse.

"No," she assures me. "And oftentimes severing the link is the best thing for both parties. Like if two people are in some kind of infinite loop. Then it helps *both* people when the bond is broken."

"It won't matter to Gabriel either way."

He was completely unmoved by the fact that I'd lost the auction. His expression had been blank, his attitude all business as he oversaw the stranger's contract with Miller Industries. I waited until the very last page was signed, on the one percent chance that his backing would fall through. That Gabriel would find some secret way to let me buy the house instead.

He was completely stoic as he signed away the house, my mother's diary inside.

"It will help Christopher," Harper says, sounding aggrieved. "He spends way too much time focusing on where I go and what I do. I bet he'll be *relieved* to cut the string."

I glance at Will. "Do you have someone picked out?"

I'm a little nervous to learn about his life. Is

there someone he's hiding from? Is that how he ended up on the streets? Someone who threatens him? There's darkness there. A history filled with shadows and violence. "Yes," he says, sounding more sad than angry. "I picked someone."

He doesn't seem inclined to say more.

"Okay," Harper says. "Hold the person in your mind. Think positive thoughts for them. You wish them well, away from you. Blowing in the wind."

She touches the bundle of weed to the flame, catching the end on fire. Then she blows it out, its embers still glowing like the end of the joint. Then she waves it around my head and down my body.

"Over your eyes," she says, as if remembering. "Your third eye. And maybe your chakras. I don't really remember, but I'll just do all of you to be sure."

I cough at the thick swell of smoke. "I'm pretty sure all this is doing is getting me really high."

Harper repeats the same motions over Will. "If you can't get rid of the bastards, being really high is the next best thing."

She waves the bundle over herself and then tosses it into the fire. The sweet scent curls around us, sharp and strong. Smoke stings my eyes, and I blink against tears.

"Now our spirits are cleansed and free. Do you feel better?"

"I might be floating," I say, squinting against the curls of smoke.

"This is some good shit," Will says, sounding impressed.

"You know what else?" I lie down on the cooler's plastic bottom, looking up at the smoky sky. "You're right. Gabriel Miller is a bad man. A very bad man. And I never want to see him again."

"Um, Avery?" Harper's voice sounds wobbly, like she's holding back a laugh.

A low growling sound comes from Will's direction.

And a face appears amid the swirling smoke. Dark bronze eyes dancing with firelight. *Gabriel.*

Chapter Fifteen

"I DON'T UNDERSTAND why you carried me. I can walk."

Gabriel sits me down on the edge of the bed, his careful movement at odds with the harsh set of his mouth. "You're high enough you'd jump off a bridge if I let you. How much weed did you smoke?"

"Barely any!" I'm indignant, even though he might be right. Has the ceiling always been spinning? It's not a troublesome dizziness, more of a pleasant whirl. The teacup ride at the carnival, lights blurred all around me. "But then Harper did the cleanse."

"The cleanse?"

"So you'd be out of my life." I frown at him. "I don't think it worked."

"What a surprise," he says drily.

"How did you find me, anyway? Outside the motel room?"

"I heard the bleating of an innocent little

lamb in a den of wolves."

"Will is a nice guy," I say defensively.

He came to stand between me and Gabriel, protecting me. I don't want Gabriel to do anything as retribution.

"I was talking about your friend."

That makes me smile. "No one else thinks she's dangerous."

"I'm good at reading people. It helps with business."

Part of me wants to know why he made a deal with my father. Did he suspect my father would cheat him? I'm afraid to hear the answers, the fallout still too fresh.

"What would you say about me?" I ask instead. "Besides being an innocent little lamb."

He sets my shoes aside and tugs my socks off, his manner brusque. "Naive. Young. Trusting."

I open my mouth to object and then see the glint in his eyes. He's teasing me, though you wouldn't know it to hear him. "I'm serious."

"You're stoned."

"Fine," I say, lying back on the bed. "I'm going to read *you*."

He gives a short laugh. "Sure."

"Asshole."

His hands work at my jeans, touch impersonal.

I slap his hands away. It's one thing for him to touch me when he's giving me pleasure, when he's taking his own. Another entirely for him to help me like I'm an invalid. I'm high, not paralyzed.

He brushes my hands aside. "Stay still."

My eyes narrow. "Controlling."

The look he gives me is pointed. "Someone has to take care of you."

"Maybe my father would do that if he wasn't in a hospital bed."

He tugs down my jeans, leaving my panties in place. "He failed you."

Anger beats against my ribs, rhythmic and ancient. How dare he? "Dangerous."

Reaching behind me, he pulls aside the covers. White sheets swirl almost psychedelic in the light from the bathroom. Maybe the smoke from the cleanse was too much.

I don't fight him as he tucks me into bed, hands gentle but firm, expression implacable. Did I hurt his feelings with what I said about him? Sometimes I wonder if he has any feelings. Maybe he's just a wild animal, acting on instinct and aggression.

Other times I think he hurts too deeply to ever let himself be vulnerable.

Reaching up, I trace my finger along his eyebrow. It feels more bushy now that I'm high, as if everything is exaggerated. Gabriel is larger and stronger. Bigger in every way.

"Read me," I whisper.

His eyes darken, almost swirling with molten gold. "Loyal."

That's nicer than I expected. "What else?"

He touches his square-tipped forefinger to the inside of my brow, smoothing the curve to my temple, reflecting my movement back to me. "Beautiful."

A flush heats my cheeks. I didn't think he would compliment me. It's shocking, embarrassing. It makes me crave even more. "One more."

His head tips forward. I only have seconds to register his intent, seconds of breathless panic and overwhelming desire, before his lips touch mine. His tongue sweeps across my lips with startling immediacy. And then he licks inside my mouth, possessive and sure. There's no hesitation with him, no question as he forces my body into full arousal.

The marijuana heightens all my senses, and with sex it's even worse. My body is on fire, burning from the inside out, a need raging so fast and so far that I don't know how he can put me out. All I know is that I need him inside me, desperately, hips rocking into the air with humiliating urgency.

"Please," I whisper.

Instead of touching me, he gives me one final word. "Mine."

It should be a shock of cold water. He doesn't have any right to me. One month. My body. That small strip of skin that he took between my legs. That's all he gets. He doesn't own me.

Except my thighs clench in helpless response, a betrayal to every fierce instinct.

"Gabriel," I whisper.

He pulls the covers over me, tucking them around my body. "Go to sleep."

"I can't. I'm too..." The flush threatens to scorch my skin, burning a path from my breasts to my neck to my cheeks. "I'm too turned on."

Any other time his expression would be priceless. This man who faces million-dollar business deals with cool efficiency, who ruthlessly destroys those who cheat him, looks worried. "You're what?"

I wriggle against the cool sheets, seeking respite and finding none. "I'm so warm. Down there. I need you to help me."

"Christ," he breathes.

There's awe in his eyes. And anger too. He's a contradiction wrapped up in one hard-packed masculine package, layers of secrets and armor. What would it be like to reach the center of him? What would I find?

"Please," I beg, reaching for his hand, moving it to the place between my legs over the covers.

"It's the pot," he says, almost to himself. "You don't want this. You don't want me."

Except I do want him. I know it's wrong to want a man who ruined my family, wrong to desire a man who purchased my body. He humiliates me just to prove a point. How can that be sexy? Except he does so with such skill that I can't help but respond, such power that my body falls under his thrall in some evolutionary equation.

He's right about one thing—my father did fail me. And Gabriel would defend his domain with a ferocity I find seductive, the sweet ache of a barbed-wire embrace.

My body presses against him, my clit throbbing with the blunt pressure of his hand. Too light. Too indistinct. I could press a pillow between my legs after he leaves, but I don't want that. Coarse fabric and a cold room. "I want you."

He thrums with tension, held frozen by invisible chains. "You're under the influence."

I always want him. In my dreams, in the dark. A secret desire I'm afraid to admit to myself. Maybe the pot loosened my control, but the feelings were always there. "It hurts."

Finally he snaps from his self-imposed restraint. "Show me."

My cheeks are burning with shame, but not enough to stop me from pushing down the blanket. My legs are bare, only the thin fabric of my panties to shield me.

His eyes blaze. "All the way, little virgin. Let me see that pretty cunt."

Shaking hands push down my panties. I press my legs together, but he shakes his head slowly. Every part of me, exposed. *His.* I belong to him, and that knowledge gives me the strength to spread my knees.

A shudder runs through his large frame. "God, Avery. That pussy. So pink. So fucking wet. It haunts me, the memory of you. I think I'd spend every second inside you if you were with me."

"You said you were done with me."

"Never. I'd never let you out of bed."

In my high state that strikes me as funny and I giggle. "Even to shower?"

"I'd shower with you. Press you up against the glass, run my hands over your skin with soap, push my cock into your heat. Hear your cries echo on the tile."

My breath catches. "Do it."

"In this place? No, I want you in my bathroom. In my bed."

Anger rises up in me, that he's toying with me. That he would send me away only to lure me back. The auction for my virginity may have been dirty, but at least it was honest.

"Tell me the real reason you sent me away. Not so I would run."

He smiles slightly, looking sinister. "You think I don't enjoy the chase?"

"You do, but that's not why you sent me away."

His hand trails down my arm, light and teasing. "Touch yourself, little virgin. Touch yourself, and I'll tell you the truth."

I shudder at the tickle of his touch, the temptation of denial. Then I smooth my hand across my tummy and down, down, down. Where I'm already wet and hot. Ready for him.

"Tell me," I whisper.

His eyes are trained on mine. "Your clit."

I touch the small bundle of nerves, and pleasure courses through me. "God."

Without looking down, his eyes darken with satisfaction. Whatever he sees, it's in my eyes. "You won't remember this. Not anything that I say."

"Then it doesn't matter."

"It matters," he says softly. "It matters that you broke down my defenses when no one else could. When I swore that I'd never let anyone close to me. Especially you."

The final words strike against my clit, rougher than my fingertip. My hips push into my hand, desperate even while my mind struggles to make sense of him. "Why me?"

He leans close. "Faster, beautiful. Harder. The way I touch you."

My hand moves without conscious thought, obeying him without question. I rub in harsh circles, building the pleasure higher, fighting an ache I can't contain.

"Why?" The word comes out as a whisper.

Then his lips are inches from my ear, breath a warm caress against my cheek. "Your father did more than fail you, little virgin. He sold you. Before you ever set foot in the Den, you were already mine."

Confusion and sensation collide, spinning

wildly like a carousel, blinding, dizzy, my body out of my control, my hands, his words, before I crash in a rainbow of blissful oblivion.

Chapter Sixteen

I WAKE UP to midafternoon light and the soft hint of music. Harper sits at the table with a textbook and a latte, earphones plugged in. And beside the textbook, a chess set. A familiar one.

I sit up, wondering how much of what I remember is a dream. The auction yesterday, the barrel of sweet-smelling fire. Strange colors lighting up the sky.

Harper pulls out her headphones. "Hello, sleepyhead."

"What's going on?"

She laughs. "I got you a chai tea."

There's a white paper cup beside me on the nightstand, and I take a fortifying sip. "God, what exactly happened last night?"

"I can't remember," she says cheerfully. "Which is really the best kind of night."

I groan. "Speak for yourself."

"Don't worry. You had a good time."

"How do you know?"

"You aren't wearing pants, for one thing."

With horror I realize that I only have panties on. When did my jeans come off? Did I take them off to sleep? Gabriel's eyes flash across my memories, and I shiver. "Oh my God."

Harper scrunches her nose. "You remember?"

"Gabriel Miller was here."

"Yeah," she says, clearly trying not to look amused. "He left a calling card."

The chess set. Not just any chess set. The chess set that he had custom carved for my arrival, the one we played with in the library. *The one he used during sex.*

Dread sinks in my stomach. I climb out of bed and walk closer, a heavy certainty slowing me down. I know what I'll find. Or rather, what I *won't* find. The pawn he used to circle my clit, faster and faster, until I came in harsh spasms.

The last I saw, that pawn lay discarded on his bedroom floor. Where was it now? On his nightstand, some kind of perverted trophy? Or thrown away, something he no longer wanted to use?

"I feel sick," I whisper.

"I did notice there's a piece missing," she says, studying the set. The pieces have been lined up on their places, as if someone is ready to play. "It's not very useful like this."

There's no way I'm going to tell her what the missing pawn means.

"Did he leave anything else?"

"Not that I know of." She shrugs. "I guess the cleansing ritual didn't work."

"The what?"

"Nothing."

I close my eyes, wishing I could remember. A little relieved that I can't. "I need to find out who bought the house. A diary won't be worth anything to them. Maybe they'll give it to me. Or I can use the trust to buy it."

"Okay," she says. "How will you find out?"

Unfortunately there's only one person who might tell me. "The same person who left this chess set."

"Can I watch?"

I narrow my eyes at her. "Don't enjoy this so much. One little phone call and your big bad stepbrother would know where you're hiding."

A gasp. "You wouldn't."

I really wouldn't, but I just give her a serene smile. If that makes her a little less gleeful about my predicament, then it's worth it. I already have to face down a lion. And I can't count on Charlotte to sneak me into his office again.

There's one place I know I can find him. The Den.

CHAPTER SEVENTEEN

I T'S ONLY BEEN three weeks since I walked down these low steps, since I stood on this rain-slicked stoop. Behind me is a dark city, the air electric with the promise of danger. Crime and sex. Mainstays of downtown Tanglewood. But I know the true risk lies in front of me. The brass ring in the lion's mouth may as well be a loaded gun. I grasp the cold metal and knock it against the base.

The heavy door nudges open an inch. My heart thuds against my chest, echoing the single knock.

The men who frequent the Den are the most powerful in the city. A thief from the street wouldn't steal from them unless they wanted swift retribution, even if the door is unlocked. But powerful men make powerful enemies, and leaving the door open feels reckless.

Unless they're expecting someone.

I hold my breath, listening intently for voices

inside. All I hear is the low buzz of traffic from behind me, the distant whine of a siren.

"Hello," I call through the slim opening.

No response.

It could be suicide to enter their space uninvited, an aggressive move to a wild animal.

What if one of those powerful enemies already forced their way inside? Someone could be hurt, bleeding, dying. I know it's an overactive imagination. No one would catch Gabriel Miller unaware. No one can touch him.

And still I don't walk away. Something draws me inside. The force of Gabriel himself, maybe, the magnetic attraction of him. My opposite. My downfall.

I step into the dark hallway, my heart beating a hundred times a minute. And with every rapid tick I'm counting down the seconds until someone discovers me. Will they pull a gun on me? Will they shoot first and ask questions later?

It's not only Gabriel who might find me. Any one of the dangerous men who visit might discover me. Any one of the ex-con security guards they employ might confront me.

"Gabriel?" I ask, my voice wavering. "Mr. Miller?"

He isn't the man I came to see that first time.

I had come to ask for a loan from Damon Scott. But I didn't have anything for collateral, so he said no. The auction was my only choice.

The silence seems to echo in my eardrums, as if I'm in a giant seashell.

Leather armchairs and ornate wooden tables stand silent witness from the spacious sitting room. A grandfather clock ticks from the end of the hall, pointing out the evening hour. Someone would be here, having a drink. Smoking a cigar. *Purchasing a virgin.* That's what they do here. That's what this place is for. So why is it empty?

"Mr. Scott?"

Before the auction Damon Scott had a photographer take pictures of me. Not naked, but almost. Wearing only my white panties and white bra, hiding my face with my hair. They were meant to generate interest in the auction among the wealthy, perverted men of the city.

Damon had only told me later that the pictures had never been circulated. Of the men at the auction, only Gabriel Miller had ever seen them.

On the first step from the bottom, something small and wooden rests.

Without touching it, I bend down to look at it. The missing pawn from the chess set. A breadcrumb to where Gabriel wants to lead me.

SKYE WARREN

And I know now, with this one small token, that this was all intentional. What his end goal is, I don't know. But he planned this. *He plans everything.*

This pawn once touched me in my most intimate place. It was once slick with my arousal.

And Gabriel Miller sucked the wetness from the curved head.

Sidestepping the pawn, I climb the steps with increasing anxiety. What does he want from me? How does he know I'll be here? But of course there's no one else I can turn to, not when I need my mother's diary.

At the top of the stairs I hesitate. I can still turn around. Back down the stairs. Out into the city. I can leave this behind—Gabriel Miller and the shameful auction. And the key to unlock my family's history.

Lifting my chin, I walk down the narrow hallway. I might as well be facing a guillotine. A firing squad. The death of any pride I have left.

The room where the photographer took my pictures has the same surreal, wavy light from my dreams. Some trick of the old windows, bubbles in the glass and ripples in the surface. The light changes color with every blink, dancing over my skin.

Except the room is empty. I take two steps inside. Where is he?

"Kneel," comes a low voice from behind me.

My breath catches. This is how it feels to be the fly in a web. Anything I do will only bind me tighter. *Will you fight me?* he asked. Because he wants to tie me down.

I kneel, the floor hard and painful beneath my knees.

He moves to stand in front of me, nothing but solidity and shadow, his white shirt open at the neck, revealing a dusting of hair. His hand clasps my neck loosely, a gentle threat. I swallow against his palm, nerves overcoming my desire to submit.

Then he curves his palm around so he's cupping me, fingers gently stroking the sensitive skin at my nape. He could hurt me like this. He could use me.

He pulls me close until my cheek rests against his thigh. It's like he's blessing me, absolving me, but how could that be possible when he's the worst sinner of all? He can't save me.

"Little virgin, do you know why your father lost his business?"

I stiffen. "Because of you. You bought it from him, and then—"

"By then it was too late for him. Only a desperate man would try to cheat the devil. How did someone with so much money lose everything?"

The question has haunted me since the trial. I blamed Gabriel Miller for the form of retaliation, but why had my father cheated him? Why had he gambled with his largest business?

Gabriel's rough fingers stroke my skin, back and forth, soothing me. "Do you want to know the answer?"

It's a fair question, because even as I'm dying to know—I'm afraid that the answer will be the end. I've stood by my father this entire time. Through the trial and the horrible press. Trading in my college fund so that he could pay restitution instead of jail time. I auctioned my virginity so that we could keep the house and pay for his medical care.

He's a good father, a good man. He doesn't deserve what Gabriel has done to him.

The entire time a quiet question echoed in my chest. *What if I'm wrong about him?*

Gabriel leans down to whisper in my ear. "Please me, and I'll tell you."

He straightens, and I know what I have to do. My fingers feel numb as I work the fastening of his pants. He's already hard inside, his cock leaning heavily from the placket once free. Impossibly hot, burning my palm. I stroke him with both hands, working him until his breath comes faster.

"Your mouth," he says roughly.

And I need some semblance of power, so I lick at the tip. I mouth the hard length of him. I press a chaste kiss to the base, where coarse hair tickles my lips.

He growls low in his throat, the vibration running down his body, through his cock. "Suck me, little virgin. Take me inside. Let me fuck those pink lips. I need to feel your throat."

His words spark a flame inside me, and it's with humiliating arousal that I slip him into my mouth. Salt smooths over my tongue, the taste of his weakness. He may not care about me, but he wasn't lying about the sex. He needs it as badly as I need answers.

He clasps his hands behind my head, murmuring, "Open for me. Open. Just a little bit. I need to use you like this. I need to—fuck, Avery."

I relax my jaw and let his cock slide deeper, the ridge slick over my tongue, the head thick in my throat. My body jerks once, resisting, but he holds me still—taking my air—until I relax. Not exactly trusting. Accepting what he does to me.

That's the only kind of prayer I know.

His hips move against me, faster now, finding his rhythm, thrusting into my mouth the same way he would between my legs. His groans are an uneven symphony, cataloging his descent.

And that same animal instinct that made me run recognizes his power. His strength. I'm subservient to him in every way, desperate for his protection, submitting to his desires. My body readies itself to ease his way—saliva coating his shaft, arousal damp between my legs.

His smooth movements grow erratic, rough thrusts startling in the dark. I choke on the length of him, but he doesn't ease up. Doesn't give me room to breathe. I have to suck in air through my nose, panicked for a moment, eyes wide open.

When he comes, it's not deep in my throat. It's with the head of his cock against my tongue, pooling salt where I'll taste it most, slick and warm. My swallow makes it disappear, but the flavor of him lingers even when he pulls away.

In the aftermath I pant, my forehead pressed to his leg, his trembling hand in my hair.

"I should hate you." My voice is hoarse, still raw from his cock.

His leg presses between mine. "It's all right, little virgin. You do."

"Then why does it feel like this?"

"Because you need to come. Like this. No one can see you."

My breath catches, because the top of his foot nudges between my legs. It's horrifying to think of coming like this, rutting against him on the floor, the taste of his come in my mouth—but now that the idea has bloomed, I can't think of anything else. My hips move on their own, rocking against him, every glance of my panties against the Italian leather of his shoes a sweet relief.

No one can see you. He sees me, every terrifying desire, every secret fear.

His hand fists in my hair, pulling me against him with the same rhythm he fucked my mouth. My body conforms to him naturally, accepting the heat and muscle of his leg in place of a real embrace, welcoming the crude stroke of his shoe in place of a caress.

"That's right," he says, voice tight. "Oh fuck, you're perfect."

Something moves by my face, and I realize it's his fist. He's stroking himself, groaning as if in pain so soon after coming, unable to help himself.

It's the spray of hot come across my cheek that triggers my own climax. I bear down on his leg, moaning with the weight of my own debasement. Pleasure sparks everywhere that he touches me—between my legs, knee pressed between my breasts, the tip of his cock sliding against my cheek. I'm made of some other material, inhuman, alight by the things that should disgust me. This man, his treatment of me. The unbearable beauty of surrender.

I'm floating in some otherworldly space. Reality can't intrude in these four walls. It can't penetrate this strange light. Distantly I hear the rustle and zip as he straightens his clothes.

Something small and white floats down in front of me.

Then he's gone from the room. I don't hear his footsteps, but I feel his presence disappear. The force of him, gone. I'm alone here. Again.

Slowly, carefully, as if recovering from a great blow, I wipe my cheek. His come is sticky and cooling against my fingers. A handkerchief. That's what he dropped at my knees. I look at the fine fabric, probably imported Italian silk. Monogrammed with the letter M with intricate scrollwork. I use it to wipe him from my skin before tossing the fabric in a small wastebasket in the hall. Discarding it like trash, the same way he left me.

As I descend the steps, I can see that the pawn isn't on the bottom step anymore.

Instead there's something rectangular. A book. Small. Leather-bound. My heart beats faster. I stumble the last steps until I can pick up my mother's diary. I hold it close to my chest, throat tight. I don't know how he got it back, whether he kept it all along or bought it from the auction winner. He teases me and toys with me, he demeans me and degrades me, but all I feel right now is gratitude. If he hadn't guaranteed the money in the escrow account, I wouldn't have been able to attend the auction. If he hadn't sent the limo early so I would have time in the house, I would never have found the diary. And if he hadn't caught me in his web, I wouldn't have the answers inside.

Chapter Eighteen

THE NEXT MORNING I visit my father, and the nurse gives me a genuine smile. "He's been awake on and off. I imagine you'll be able to talk to him today."

My heart thuds in anticipation. He used to be my rock, my sole family member after the loss of my mother years ago. And he never remarried—never wanted to, that was how much he loved her. So it was just the two of us, playing chess or hosting society events in the ballroom. Now here we are—me living out of a cheap motel, him bedridden on the charity of his sworn enemy.

"Daddy, can you hear me?"

His eyelids flutter, but after a moment he goes still again. Sleeping. Disappointment wars with relief inside me. I desperately want my ally back, my family, but I know that even he can't be that. He needs me to give him support. He doesn't have any left himself.

I leave the book of history on the table and

pull out the diary. I stayed up late last night, reading from the beginning. One story of her and Nina Thomas sneaking out of a coming-out ball to take a canoe across the lake had me giggling through my tears. She wasn't quite as proper of a lady as I was told, but that only makes me love her more.

She longed for adventure before she settled into her role as a society wife.

I flip through the pages filled with her elegant, now-familiar scrawl.

And the man I truly want has no money, no standing. No chance of winning my hand. We both know that it's impossible, but the heart doesn't believe in boundaries.

Who was this mystery man? Did my father ever know him?

I flip ahead to a part I haven't read yet, where she's engaged to Daddy, and read aloud.

"'Mother wants the best of everything. The flowers. The cake. Anything less will seem like we can't afford it, and that would be vulgar. Of course the truth is that we can't afford it, but Geoffrey graciously agreed to cover everything. He says we'll share everything in a few months anyway.'"

That sounds like Daddy, incredibly generous.

Completely in love.

Whatever happened with the mystery man, it hadn't changed her decision.

"'It seems like there's a party every week. Officially I attend with Mother, and sometimes Father, but I always know that Geoffrey will be there. He does make me laugh.'" A smile touches my lips. "You make me laugh too, Daddy."

But he must have smiled more before my mother died. There was always a tinge of sadness to him, as if he couldn't stop remembering her.

The fact that I looked so similar just made it harder for him. I shudder as I remember Uncle Landon's marriage proposal, the way I would have been a replacement for her. Disturbing. *Disgusting*. There's a difference between wanting someone and loving someone. For my father, who genuinely loved my mother, the likeness had been a sad reminder of what he would never get back.

I turn the page. "'Tonight he asked me to sneak to the boat house with him. I know he wanted to kiss me. Maybe more. I told him I couldn't risk leaving, that we might be caught.'"

That gives me pause. I know that she sneaked out with Nina Thomas. Multiple times based on the way she described their antics. So why had she lied to Daddy back then?

But it was still a big deal to be alone with a boy then, especially in high society. It was even a big deal now in the upper echelons of Tanglewood. Girls like me were supposed to attend women-only universities, to get a nice degree in something demure, like ancient mythology, before marrying a nice boy like Justin. And only then should we have sex, according to the strict boundaries laid out by society matrons. That would have been my life. I would have gone into that darkness willingly, never knowing that the nice boys purchased women at dark-room virginity auctions. At least Gabriel Miller is honest about his intentions.

"'He asked me where I want to go for my honeymoon,'" I read over the gentle drone of the machines. "'I told him it doesn't matter. As long as we're together I can be happy anywhere.' Well, you guys were just too adorable. I love it."

My father murmurs something indistinct, eyes still closed.

"Can you hear me, Daddy? Do you recognize her words? I feel so much closer to her, reading this. I know her so much better. Like I can hear her voice in my head."

No response. I hold back a sigh. He might not wake up, despite what the nurse said.

"'And so he told me that we're going to Greece.'" I stumble over the last word. All the times I had talked about mythology, all the times I had dreamed of visiting the ruins, he never told me he'd been. "'He said I'm the most beautiful woman in the world, his very own Helen of Troy. We'll leave right after the wedding, that very night.'"

My father's head thrashes side to side. His mutters grow louder, more disturbed. Something's bothering him. Is he in pain? But the nurse said he was doing better today.

I lean closer. "Daddy, what's wrong?"

He makes a low keening sound. The hair on my neck rises.

"Oh God," I whisper. "Can you hear me? Is it hearing about Mama that's hurting you?"

"Helen," he says, like last time.

"I'm sorry, Daddy. I thought you would like hearing her diary, but I'll stop."

His eyes flutter open. Confusion clouds his eyes. "Helen?"

"It's me, Avery. I'm here."

Slowly he focuses on me, eyes bright with tears. "There you are, my girl. I've missed you."

For months I took care of him every day. Feeding him. Bathing him. I couldn't afford the kind of full-time care he needed, so I did it myself. And it brought us closer, even if it was the hardest thing I've ever done.

"I'm sorry."

"Where did you go?"

The day of the auction, two weeks ago, I left the house and never came back. Gabriel Miller hired a full-time nurse to compensate. But Daddy would know I was gone.

"I didn't want to leave, but I had to do something. I was trying to…" I swallow past my grief. "I was trying to save the house. I'm so sorry, Daddy. It didn't work."

His eyebrows press together. "Your mother?"

"I know. She left me the house in trust. But Uncle Landon… I'm sorry. I know you were friends with him, but he borrowed from my trust." He stole from it, the way Daddy stole from Gabriel Miller. "And when it ran out of money, the court took away the house."

"How?" His voice is rough from disuse. "How are you paying?"

I realize he means the nursing home. He knew we couldn't afford full-time care before. Now he's in the most exclusive facility in the city.

I can't bring myself to say Gabriel Miller's name right now, not so soon after confessing that we lost the house. "Someone is helping me pay for it. Don't worry, Daddy."

Sorrow fills his eyes. He doesn't know the illicit details, but he can guess. "My good girl."

It was the same thing he said to me after I bested him in chess. He always looked more proud after I beat him than when he would win. Except I haven't won this game. I've lost.

Chapter Nineteen

HARPER AND I order a pizza with everything on it. *If we're not getting wasted, let's at least load up on carbs and dairy.* A movie beneath static on the small TV.

"I didn't even know there was still this kind of station, like it's not cable."

I finish off the crust on my third slice. "Me neither. It's kind of fun not having a guide station. Or really having that many things to choose from. You get what you get."

"Like Chatroulette meets Netflix."

A snort escapes me. "We are truly ridiculous."

She leans back against the headboard. "And stuffed. I'm done."

I peek under the lid of the box. "There's still half a pizza in here. We should offer it to Will."

"I already invited him inside when the pizza guy came. He told me to fuck off."

He isn't winning any personality awards, but I have a soft spot for the guy who spends most of the time outside my door. He has a lost quality, as if he's waiting for something he knows will never come. He's not waiting for half of a cheap pizza, but it's all I offer him outside the door.

With a reluctant nod of thanks he accepts the box, still sitting against the building.

"Are you sure you don't want to come inside? We're watching Meg Ryan and Tom Hanks be cute together."

"*Sleepless in Seattle?*"

"*You've Got Mail.*"

He shakes his head. "Those kinds of movies piss me off."

"Ones with happy endings?"

"Ones with rich people," he says roughly.

Okay then. I duck back into the room and curl into bed beside Harper. I'm not looking forward to when she goes back to school. Mostly we don't talk about it, preferring to trade insults and threats instead. I know she's here partly to escape her own demons—namely, her stepbrother. But it's been an incredible solace to have someone on my side during this time.

A true friend, the kind my mother had.

We watch Meg Ryan struggle to save her store, only to lose everything.

"This is hitting a little close to home," I say.

"Yeah, but she had that store for so long. You have your whole life ahead of you. A career. A family. All that jazz. This is not the end."

"This is not the end," I repeat, tasting the words. It's comforting. "I think I need to get that tattooed on me somewhere so I don't forget."

"But how awkward will it be once it *is* the end and you've still got a tattoo that's wrong."

A loud knock comes from the door.

I glance at her. "Did you order another pizza?"

She shakes her head. "I'm never eating again."

"Maybe Will changed his mind about the movie."

I open the door to find a standoff outside. Tension radiates from the bodies of three different men, violence simmering in the air. Will stands in front of the door, blocking my view. In the narrow space between his arm and the doorframe I can see Justin standing there, blue eyes blazing, dark shadows beneath making him look sinister.

And behind him I recognize Harper's stepbrother, looking just as fierce. Christopher has a clean-cut style that's completely betrayed by the coldness of his eyes. He's warm enough to me, but when it comes to his stepsister his temperature drops below zero. Where Gabriel Miller is a lion, wild and golden, Christopher's is a sleek panther with dark eyes and black hair.

"Uh, Harper?"

"Who is it?" she asks, digging through the makeup bag that has her nail polish. "And what do you think about Helter-Skelter as a color? It matches my mood."

"You better come here. Things are about to get weird."

CHAPTER TWENTY

IT TAKES A few taut minutes to convince Will that these guys aren't going to hurt us. At least, not physically. Both of them have the power to wreck us emotionally, though Harper would swear that isn't true. But she looks pale as Christopher demands to know why she didn't return his calls.

"And why hasn't your phone been on?"

Her eyes narrow. "How do you know it's been off?"

"Because I had it traced," he says flatly. "And there was no signal. None at all."

"I can't believe you had me tracked like an animal! And that's why it was off. Because you're insane."

"I wouldn't have to track you if you didn't do this." He makes a rough slash with his hand.

"Do what?"

"Run off to the slums with your friend in some kind of psychotic sleepover."

"Harsh," I say, stung on her behalf.

He gives me a hard look before turning back to Harper. "We'll discuss this outside. Alone."

Then they leave, and it's only Justin and me in the shitty hotel room. There's a half-empty bottle of Coke on the nightstand. Textbooks stacked with fashion magazines on the small table. Psychotic sleepover isn't that far off.

"God, Avery," Justin says, his voice lower than I remember. Overall he looks harder, leaner. He's always been fit; being captain of the rowing team has its compensations.

But there was a boyishness to his face. That's gone now.

"I've been looking for you," he says, sounding tormented.

I shift, uncomfortable. "You know it's over between us."

"I made a mistake," he says, taking my hand. "When I found out about your father, thinking about what it would do for my career. Then my dad making his fucking ultimatums."

My heart squeezes in remembered grief as I'd realized how little I meant to him. We had said *I love you* to each other. We had promised to marry each other. And he had turned his back at the first sign of trouble.

"It was a difficult time for everyone," I say, trying to be kind. It's for the best that we found out then that we wouldn't work out. Better that than finding out after we said *I do.*

"I had time to think about it." He stalks away, muttering a curse. "And then the auction."

One night at Gabriel's house Justin showed up—at my window, no less. Like some knight in shining armor. That's the thing about a knight whose armor shines, though. It's never been in battle. Never been tested. Tarnished black armor like Gabriel's—that's where strength lies.

Looking at Justin now, he does seem harder than before. Stronger.

He turns to face me, his expression resolute. "Avery, I know I failed you before. I love you, and I let you down. I'm going to make it up to you, if you'll let me. And I'll never leave you again."

I take an instinctive small step back, dismayed by the strange allure of him. He represents my old life, the one I've left behind. A small voice whispers, *you'll get some of it back.*

"I don't know," I say, shaking my head.

"Just talk to me," he says, voice low. "Sit with me. Don't kick me out. That's all I'm asking. I know we have a long way to go until you trust me again."

I look down, on the verge of unexpected tears. Even with Harper here I've been so desperately alone. Facing Gabriel, who plays chess like a grand master. And I'm fumbling every turn.

The promise of a friend is so tempting.

"Okay," I say, voice breaking. "Let's talk."

"Thank you," he says, earnest and impossibly handsome. He looks older with a five o'clock shadow across his jaw, his hair tousled instead of neatly cropped.

He pulls something from his pocket and holds it out.

I open it, blinking at what I see. The deed to a house. In Washington. "What? But how—"

"My father disowned me," he says, speaking faster. "I told him I wasn't going to give you up. Even though I didn't know if you'd ever accept me again, I wanted him to know."

"Oh my God, Justin."

"From there I went to the senator who opposed my father. He lost because he didn't play dirty. But I know all my father's tricks."

My eyes widen. "You're going to help someone win against him?"

"No, Avery. I'm going to run against him. I'm going to win."

My mouth opens. And closes.

I struggle to take in what he's telling me. "But I don't understand. The next election isn't for two years. And how did you get money for a house if your father disowned you?"

"I made a deal with the party. Told them enough so they'd know I was serious. Kept enough back so they'd still need me. And I got an advance on my percentage of the ad buys."

Shock stops my heart. "No," I whisper.

"Yes," he says forcefully. "I know you wanted your mother's house. I couldn't get that one, but we can build a life in this one. A new family."

"A family," I repeat faintly.

"I needed to show you that I'm serious about this, about us. I need you to know you can trust me now. I'll never leave you again. We can leave this behind."

I know I should be moved that Justin chose me after all, grateful that he made this gesture even if it wasn't the one I wanted. But even while I hold the piece of paper, so thin for a document this important, all I can think about is Gabriel— the way he tucked me in. The way he made me kneel. Gestures that moved me deeper than I thought possible.

CHAPTER TWENTY-ONE

IN THE NEXT few hours the landscape of my room changes drastically. Christopher insists that Harper leave the motel. Any of the ritzy hotels will suffice. Harper wants me to come with her, but I decline for the same reason that I wouldn't go with Justin. I want to survive on my own, however painful it is. And it's pretty painful watching my friend pack her stuff.

"Come with me," she says again, eyes imploring.

"I think you just want me as a shield," I tease her. "I don't think Christopher's that bad."

"Um, whose side are you on? He's awful. And I wouldn't turn down a shield. Or an entire fortress and drawbridge even. But I want you to come because you're my friend."

Impulsively I reach for her, enclosing her slender frame in my arms. "It's good he came for you. You don't belong here."

"You don't either," she says, grasping my arms

and giving me a little shake.

Maybe the old Avery James didn't belong here. The new Avery doesn't belong anywhere.

I force a smile. "Text me."

"Like every other minute."

And then she's gone in a black sedan, leaving me with a solemn Justin. He offered to take me to a hotel, too. Apparently he's here on secret business, meeting with some Tanglewood businesspeople for fundraising purposes. That means he has a suite at the Ritz.

He's made a deal with the devil. We have that in common now.

"You don't have to stay," I tell him.

"I'd like to," he says. "If you want me to leave, I'll get another room, but I'd feel better watching over you."

I glance at the double bed with its rumpled sheets. It was one thing to lie in bed with Harper, watching old movies until we pass out sprawled on top of the covers. Another thing to share a bed with the boy I would have married, the one who dumped me. The one who wants me back.

And the strangest part is that it feels like a betrayal to Gabriel Miller.

His hold on me is horrible and inescapable.

"We won't do anything," Justin says, following my look. "I'll sleep on top of the covers. With my clothes on."

I can't find it in my heart to send him away, not when he's trying so hard. And maybe there is a chance for us. I loved things about him once—his generosity, the way he made me laugh. Come to think of it, I loved the same things about him that my mother loved in my father.

So that's how I end up under the sheets, my body frozen in place as the next-door neighbor does her business. Neither Justin nor I have moved for fifteen entire minutes—I've been counting. But there's no way he's asleep. No way I can sleep with the moaning happening behind us.

"Spread them," a coarse voice says. "Yeah. Fuck. Wider."

I'm sure my face would be beet red with embarrassment. At least the lights are off, leaving only the pale wash of moonlight through the curtains.

The banging grows louder and more forceful, vibrations running through the wall and into the loose bed frame we're in. God. "I'm sorry," I whisper. "You can leave if you want."

"No," he says, his voice strangled. "It's... Does this happen every night?"

"Pretty much."

"Why is it…" He swallows audibly. "For so long?"

I want to sink into the ground. "There are…multiple men. I think it's her job."

"Oh."

The silence grows until it's a dark presence in the room, a counterpoint to the wild sex noises coming from across the wall. I feel like I can barely breathe, the awareness of what's happening stealing the air. And the worst part is that I can feel Justin move, ever so slightly, as if he's uncomfortable, as if he can't help himself.

Finally he sits up and faces me, his expression hidden in shadows. "Avery, I can't hold this in anymore. You're the most beautiful woman I've ever known. I want you so much."

I scoot back against the headboard. "What are you doing?"

"I know your first sexual experience was scary, but I swear I would be gentle with you. Let me take care of you. I'll show you how it can be when you love someone."

My mouth drops open. "What are you talking about?"

"Gabriel Miller," he says, the name infused with hate. "He hurt you."

"He didn't." At least not the way Justin's

implying, with sex.

"I can see it, Avery. The way you shrink away when you think I might touch you. At least you used to let me kiss you without looking scared."

"We were engaged then."

"And we could be again. We *should* be. We belong together."

"What does that even mean?"

"We come from the same world. Gabriel Miller shouldn't even be allowed to touch you. And that he took your virginity. Fuck, Avery. Sometimes I want to—"

"Don't. You don't get to defend my honor. Not after you left me."

He relents with a rough sound. "I deserve that."

The words come tumbling out of me. "And Gabriel Miller has his faults, but he's always been honest. In his own way he's even tried to help me."

Something holds me back from telling him about my mother's diary. As if it's too private to share with Justin. *But not too private for Gabriel Miller.*

"Help you? Jesus, Avery. You can't be that naive."

The words hit me like a slap. "I'm not."

"You really don't know, do you? I wondered if Harper told you."

My blood runs cold. "Told me what?"

"The pictures, Avery. The naked pictures of you. Everyone in the city has seen them."

I scramble out of bed, bumping into the nightstand in my desperation. Walking backward until I hit the wall. "You're lying to me."

"I saw them." His laugh cuts through the distance, bitter and toxic. "More of you than I ever saw when we were engaged. How messed up is that?"

I close my eyes. "Stop."

"No, you're the one who needs to stop. Defending Gabriel Miller? He used you. He bought you, and then he *sold* you in the form of pictures to the entire city. Everyone's looking at them."

My hands go to my ears in a hopeless attempt to block him out. Tears leak from between my eyelids. This feeling of betrayal shouldn't be here. Of course Gabriel would do this. We're enemies. Not lovers. And definitely not friends.

Those pictures we took upstairs, before the auction. And Damon assured me that the pictures weren't released then. Which means Gabriel Miller only shared them after he took my virginity, once I was ruined beyond usefulness.

One final blow to my family.

Justin pulls my hands away, his expression less angry. Still fierce. "It's okay, Avery. I understand why you did it. And I forgive you."

"You...what?"

"I won't hold it against you. We can still get married."

The only thing worse than being hurt by your enemy? Being hurt by someone you once considered a friend. "Get out, Justin."

He pulls back, confusion warring with denial. "What?"

"You forgive me? I didn't ask for your forgiveness. And I definitely didn't need your permission." I may not launch a thousand ships, but I can damn well defend myself. "If you can't be there when I need you, then you don't get to be here when I don't. Leave."

Only when he shuts the door behind him do I shatter.

Chapter Twenty-Two

"DADDY!"

He's already awake when I enter the room, his face pale but eyes lively. "My good girl."

I lean over the bed and wrap him in a hug, careful not to disturb the wires all around him. He smells like alcohol and soap, but he's here—solid and alive. "I'm so glad you're awake."

"More than awake. I went for a walk today."

"What? Seriously?"

He chuckles. "For all of five minutes in the hall. The nurse helped me."

"That's amazing. You're going to be walking by yourself soon. I just know it."

"Maybe so. I feel like Rip Van Winkle. I've been asleep for decades, it feels like. What's happened with you? You look thin. Are you eating well?"

I haven't eaten since Justin left my motel room two days ago. I kept up the facade in texts to Harper, not wanting her to worry about me.

And a little hurt that she knew about the pictures and didn't tell me.

"I'm fine, Daddy. And look what I found." I hold up the diary triumphantly.

His face turns impossibly whiter, almost like concrete. "What's that?"

"It was Mama's. I found it in the attic. I've been reading it a little at a time, savoring it. And it's so amazing to hear things in her own words. About her family. And about you, too."

Something flickers across his expression. "Are you sure that's a good idea?"

Surprise makes me freeze. "What do you mean?"

"Some things are better left in the past, Avery. Your mother was a beautiful woman. The kind that every man wanted. I loved her with everything I had, but I wasn't blind to her faults."

This is the first he's mentioned of her faults. My fingers clench the worn leather as if he's ripping the diary away from me. I won't let him.

"What will I find?" I ask softly.

His dark eyes harden to obsidian. "You would speak to me that way? Especially after the secrets you've been keeping?"

Breath rushes out of my lungs. "Secrets?"

"I demanded to know who was paying for the

room. And they told me it was coming from your trust. Your trust, which I already know you drained to pay my restitution and medical bills. Which means you sold the house. How could you?"

He thinks I voluntarily sold the house to cover his stay here. That's a much more innocent explanation than the real one. "But I have her diary, Daddy. Isn't that better? Her own words."

"Words can be misleading."

Apprehension settles in my chest. How can a diary be misleading? She wrote it with no intention that it would be read. She'd have no reason to lie. The only person who had a motivation to lie about the past would be Daddy. His words could have misled me. He had certainly never mentioned a rival to my mother's hand in marriage.

"Did my mother see anyone besides you? Before you were married?"

His eyes widen. "Don't you dare speak about her that way."

"It's not an insult to her, Daddy." But whatever is inside this diary may very well indict my father. Justin called me naive when it came to Gabriel Miller, but I'm beginning to wonder if the monsters in disguise weren't around me all along.

He softens. "I just don't want you to be disappointed. I'd rather you remember her as I do, as the beautiful woman I loved."

"She's more than just the way she looked." And I am, too.

"I know that, but she was troubled."

"What does that mean?"

"You're right that she saw someone else. I didn't find out until later. Until the night before we were married. I couldn't sleep I was so excited to be with her. So I went to her room and saw her sneaking out the window."

"Oh no," I whisper.

"She was going to meet another man."

"I'm so sorry, Daddy."

"Don't be," he says, more fierce than I've seen him in years. "She married me, understand? She chose me."

"Yes." Tears sting my eyes. "She did."

"And I didn't hold it against her, but I'm not proud of it either. She said goodbye to him, said goodbye to that kind of thinking. And she was faithful to me."

"I believe you."

And I do believe him, because I can already tell from the entries what she plans to do. She's in the process of saying goodbye. That night I read the next few entries, slowly, painfully reliving the way she planned the wedding, both a new beginning and a sad farewell.

He waited for me at the theater, closed for the season and empty except for the two of us. He asked me to leave with him, to make a new life. I would never see my family again. Never see Nina again. And my family would be disgraced. I told him no.

I'll find my own happiness, here in Tanglewood.

Chapter Twenty-Three

I N THE MORNING I take a cab instead of the bus. The routes don't go into the upscale part of Tanglewood, where the gates are high and the pools are glittering. I slip the taxi driver a little extra to cruise the wide streets until I spot the house from memory. Daddy and I attended Nina Thomas's fiftieth birthday party a while ago, but I still remember the gorgeous Corinthian columns across the front.

It isn't Nina who answers the door, or even a servant, but Charlotte. Her pretty eyes widen. "Avery. Are you okay?"

That tells me what I look like right now, dark shadows under my eyes and soul grieving my father's secret shame. "I'm not sure. I'm sorry to just show up like this, but I was wondering if it would be possible to see your mother."

The worry doesn't fade from her eyes. There's curiosity too. "I'm sure she'll be happy to see you. Come in, come in."

She pulls me into a glittering foyer that opens to a large spiral staircase. To the side I can see a long dining room table with a laptop and papers covering the gleaming wood.

Charlotte gives a little laugh. "I'm always working. I have a condo near the office, but I like to come here on the weekends to spread out."

I manage a smile, but she doesn't seem to expect pleasantries. "Wait here a sec," she says, apologetic. "Let me just make sure she's up for visitors."

While she's gone, my gaze strays again to the pile of papers. Probably whoever bought my house is somewhere in that stack. Only a few yards away from me. It's a betrayal of trust to even consider looking, especially when Charlotte has been so helpful and gracious to me. I'm desperate enough to think about it, though.

A dark voice reminds me, *Other people don't play by the rules, do they?*

The dark voice sounds uncomfortably like Gabriel Miller's. The man who shared pictures of me, even after the auction was over. To humiliate me? Mission accomplished.

Charlotte skips down the steps. "She definitely wants to see you, but..." Her eyes mist over. "She has hard days sometimes. Today is one of those days."

My chest tightens. "I can come back."

"No! She'd feel awful if you left. She really does want to see you." A melancholy expression crosses Charlotte's face. "I don't think you know how much she loved your mother."

"Okay, if you're sure."

And that's how I end up in a dimly lit room smelling of incense. Wall hangings in jewel tones and damask patterns give the room an intimate feeling. A large bed sits on a platform, but it's empty. A large fireplace crackles from the side of the room, with two cream-colored armchairs perched nearby.

Nina Thomas looked ageless on her fiftieth birthday, hair and makeup flawless, not a wrinkle that could be seen. Her smile had been brilliant and white, a contrast to her smooth dark skin.

She looks like a different woman now—tired and sad. Frail despite her full body. A large-knit throw covers her legs. Is this how she looks on all her bad days? Or has that much changed in the past couple of years?

"Ms. Thomas?"

"I told you, dear," she admonishes. "Call me Nina. No Ms. Thomas and definitely no ma'am."

I'm pleased at the small show of her old spirit.

I perch on the other armchair. "Are you sure it's a good day to visit? I'm sorry I dropped by unannounced. I really can come back."

"Nonsense. A child of Helen Lancaster is always welcome here."

My mother's maiden name. A smile touches my lips. "You were the best of friends, weren't you?"

She nods toward the leather-bound book clutched in my lap. "If you've been reading that, then you know as much. There was no better woman than your mother."

Grief weighs down my heart that I didn't know her better. She was the person who cuddled me when I got sick, the person who taught me how to apply lipstick when I begged at age eight. I knew her as a mother, but I never got to know her as a woman.

"Can you…tell me about her?"

A sigh of acquiescence, fond and sad. "Of course she was beautiful. I'm sure people have told you."

I nod. "We had her portrait above the fireplace."

"You look like her. I'm sure people have told you that, too." She studies me with a critical eye. "You're softer than her. Sweeter. She had a hardness about her."

I remember that much, the way she could be kind and stern at the same time.

Nina's dark eyes turn distant. "She was smart, which you weren't supposed to be back then as a girl. Maybe not even now. With a sharp wit. You didn't want to get on her bad side."

That makes me laugh unaccountably. That there was some fault of hers, something still endearing to those who loved her. "Were you ever on her bad side?"

"Oh, plenty. Her family didn't like me. Said I was a bad influence. They were right." A husky laugh. "I was what people called a hell-raiser back then."

"I bet you could still raise hell if you wanted," I say kindly.

She grins, unrepentant. "True enough. But I think Helen wanted to break out, you know? She had been good for so long, done all the things her mother asked. And she was looking down the barrel of a life as a society wife. When would she have time to be herself except right then? About the same age you are now, I think."

An ache beats in my heart, steady and familiar. I know what it feels like to do what's expected of me, to see the future stretch in front of me. To have fleeting moments of freedom.

I hold up the diary. "I read about the canoe."

"Oh yes. Her father was furious when we dragged ourselves out of the lake, dripping wet and laughing. Who ever heard of a canoe catching fire? In the middle of the water, no less." She shakes her head, chuckling. "At least it destroyed the evidence of what we were doing."

Hesitation traps my next words, but I need to know. "There was a man she talked about. Someone who wasn't my father."

Grief presses down on her. "Yes, dear."

"Do you know…do you know who it was?"

Nina studies the fire, rubbing her hand as if her joints ache. "Are you sure you want to go down that path?"

"Daddy warned me away, too. Told me not to read the rest of the diary."

And now that I think about it, Gabriel Miller had warned me. *Did you consider that I might be protecting you? You might not like what you find inside.* I hadn't believed him then, but he might have been telling the truth. What poison does this book hold inside?

Nina's dark eyes reflecting the flames. "Do you know that I loved your mother?"

That's what Charlotte said downstairs. "I

know."

"No, I don't think you do. I loved her. Not as a friend."

My heart beats faster. Not the way that I care about Harper. "You mean, romantically?"

She nods.

"Did she love you back?"

"I think she did in her own way." Her gaze is direct. "We were lovers. It would have been scandalous back then, but no one suspected. Not even her parents thought we were anything but friends."

I don't think Tanglewood high society has changed that much. It would be scandalous now. "Wow. I never knew that. She didn't—"

She didn't mention that she was intimate with Nina, but maybe she was being careful. But then again, she said things her parents wouldn't have approved of. So why hadn't she mentioned it?

Sorrow and acceptance flit across Nina's face. "It didn't mean the same thing to her. It was a way to rebel against her parents. Something to do for fun."

"No, I'm positive she cared about you."

"Oh, she did. But I loved her with all my heart and soul. I knew we'd both have to get married, but we'd still be friends. No one would suspect what we did after, either, and I wanted it to continue."

I blush, feeling strange talking about my mother's private relations. Love is one thing. Sex is something else. Gabriel Miller taught me that. "She didn't?"

She gestures toward the diary in my hands. "Not once she met your mystery man."

"She loved him?"

A nod. "All the way. She thought about running away with him."

"And he wasn't my daddy." I already know from the diary entries, but I need to be sure. This must be what Daddy didn't want me to find. I know she didn't run away with him. She married Daddy, after all. But something happened to make her stay.

"No, he wasn't."

"Did Daddy know?"

"Not at first. There were a lot of boys in this town who wanted to marry Helen Lancaster. She would smile her Mona Lisa smile at them, and they'd think they had a chance. The only boy in the running was ever Geoffrey. Your grandmother made sure of that."

"Because he had money."

"He didn't just have money. He had an ungodly amount of money. And your grandmother had expensive tastes. Big ambitions. Nothing less would do." She laughs without humor. "And it's ironic, isn't it? The man she made your mother marry is flat broke. And the man she wanted to marry did well for himself."

"I really need to know who it was." Did she mention his name somewhere in this book?

"It wouldn't have been enough for Maeve Lancaster," Nina says, still lost in the past. "She wanted standing, too. The kind that only an established family can give you."

The kind that Justin had, at least before his father disowned him. "Please tell me."

She shakes her head. "It's not a good idea to go digging in the past. I heard they auctioned the house. You need to stay away from it."

Confusion tenses my brow. "I don't own it anymore. Why would I go there?"

Her gaze holds a warning. "Whatever you read, Avery. Don't go back."

My fingers clench around the diary, resolve thick in my throat. "I don't have any plans to step foot in that house again. But I need to find out what happened."

"Why?"

I consider that a moment, wanting to be honest with her. "Because I lived in her house for most of my life. I listened to Daddy talk about her. It's like everything I knew was a shrine dedicated to her, but it turns out I didn't know her at all."

"She had her share of secrets."

"And because…" My voice catches. "I think in some ways I might be following in her footsteps. And maybe seeing how she settled down, how she found happiness might help me do the same."

"There's a flaw in your thinking, dear."

"What's that?"

"You're assuming Helen Lancaster ever found happiness."

Foreboding runs through me in tangible, almost violent shudders.

A racking cough overtakes Nina. I kneel at her side, clasping her hand. "Is there something I can do?"

"Charlie," she says, eyes closed, leaning back.

I rush downstairs. "Charlotte? I think Nina needs you."

Charlotte comes out of the dining room, a grim look on her face. "That's another reason why I like to spend my weekends here. She doesn't like to ask for help, but she needs it."

"I'm sorry," I whisper. "I might have worn her out."

"Don't worry. Talking about Helen always does her good. And she was thrilled when I told her you had come." Charlotte bites her lip. "I'm not sure she'll be able to talk more, though. Once the exhaustion sets in—"

"Please don't worry about me. I'll show myself out."

"Okay, thank you. Do come back and visit her. I'm positive she would want to see you again." Charlotte looks relieved before she hurries up the stairs.

I watch her as she disappears into the top landing. The barest hint of voices trickles down the curving staircase. In my mind I see Charlotte hovering over her mother, Nina insisting that she's fine despite the fact that she isn't. Not entirely unlike me and my father, until the secrets started spilling out. Does Charlotte know that her mother was once lovers with mine?

My hand is on the bronze doorknob when I turn sideways.

The stack of papers is a mirage in the desert, the promise of safety. I know that whatever I find there won't save me, but I can't stop from walking into the dining room. There are demons that drive me just as they drive Gabriel to seek revenge, to demand the truth.

I take one final glance at the stairway. Empty. Complete silence.

My gaze runs over the papers that I can see. Unfamiliar addresses. Names I haven't heard before. There's so much information here. I'm not sure I can narrow it down to a single case in the few minutes I'll have to look.

I sit down in the formal dining chair at the head of the table, the embroidered cloth still warm from Charlotte's body. The laptop screen still shows her e-mail application.

My gaze snaps to Gabriel Miller's name. A double-click.

The previous owner of the home may request information about the winner of the auction. Under no circumstances should you provide it.

Heat floods my cheeks. That's how much he wants to block me, that he would send a memo?

I know that you have discretion, but I also know your family has a personal connection to this case. I trust that it won't interfere.

And now remorse burns a hole in my stomach.

I'm exploiting that personal connection right now. And I don't stop.

To underscore the importance, know that this is a privacy issue as well as a safety concern. My concern is for the well-being of Ms. James in light of the recent events.

"Avery?"

I stand up, guilt warring with anger. "What recent events?"

Her dark eyes flash. "You shouldn't have done that."

"And you shouldn't be talking about me with Gabriel Miller, pretending like it's just business when we both know it's personal."

She looks away. "This whole damn city is like a damn Greek tragedy."

"Tell me what event he's talking about."

"Shit." Her eyes close, and she gives a little shake of her head. When she meets my gaze again, she's frank and unafraid, so much like Nina. Is this how I look to people who knew my mother? "Someone vandalized the house."

"What?" Grief squeezes my heart.

"Gabriel will freak out if I tell you, but maybe you should know." She digs through some of the papers to a file folder at the bottom of a stack. "It's not like whoever did this can't find you."

Pictures appear, large and crude. The front of the house with *WHORE* written across the front door in bright red spray paint. *SLUT* scrawled above the fireplace in the empty space where my mother's portrait used to be. And in my bedroom, taped to the walls beside pictures of kittens and boy bands, are black-and-white pictures. Blown up, grainy like from an old security camera. My eyes, my lips. Breasts that could be mine.

Except I never took my bra off for the photographer.

So where did these pictures come from? The truth hits me like a sledgehammer. Gabriel didn't just share pictures that we took that day at the Den. He must have taken secret shots of me while I was at his house. When I showered, when I changed my clothes. When we had sex.

CHAPTER TWENTY-FOUR

T HE DOOR TO the Den doesn't swing open when I knock this time. No one's expecting me, but I'm damn well going to come inside. My righteous fury is almost enough to burn down the building. I'm trembling in the cold as I wait with barely leashed rage.

It's Damon Scott who opens the door, the man I went to for a loan, the one who auctioned me. "Avery. Are you all right?"

A bitter laugh breaks from me. "You're the second person to ask me that today."

"I heard what happened, and—"

"Is he here? I know he is." I push my way past Damon Scott, ready to be a bulldozer if I need to be. Or even a goddamn tank. I'm ready for war. "Gabriel?"

Smoke rises for the circle of men reclining in leather chairs. Dangerous men, all of them powerful, many of them armed. I feel no fear as I face them.

"Where's Gabriel?"

Some of them look amused, others annoyed. I recognize Ivan from the auction. He gives a cool glance toward the stairs. With a short nod of thanks, I take them two at a time.

Now I understand how Gabriel felt when he took down my father. There's a burning hunger inside me, to smash things, to ruin them—and that's exactly what I plan to do.

Gabriel Miller will be broken by the time I'm done with him. He'll beg me to stop.

There's only one piece of furniture left in the strange-light room. A chair, plain and made of wood. That's where Gabriel sits, expression haunted as he stares at a stack of papers in his hand. Before I even reach him, I know what he's seeing. My defilement.

My shame.

He looks up, and I see the bone-deep weariness in his eyes that matches my own. It's the kind that comes from a lifetime of secrets, of darkness. Of pretending they can't hurt you when you're already bleeding. It doesn't soften me toward him in the slightest. I'll twist the knife if I have to.

"Avery," he mutters, and I'm not sure I've ever heard him say my name before.

I won't let that soften me either.

"You asshole," I say, trembling with anger. "I knew you were dirty and underhanded. I knew you would purchase a woman rather than winning one the honorable way. But this?"

His brows lower. "Who told you?"

"Where do I even start? You have so many secrets and all of them are vile. Just like you."

"It might help if you explain," he says tightly. "So I know what we're discussing when you insult me."

"Insult you?" I'm almost breathless with indignation. "Insult *you?* Fine. I'll explain what I'm talking about. We'll play that game as if you *don't* know that my house was vandalized."

"Charlotte."

"Charlotte. That's all you have to say about that? That you e-mailed her specifically to tell her *not* to tell me. Conspiring with her to keep me in the dark. For what?"

"Well, because—" His eyes narrow. "How do you know what I e-mailed her? I can't imagine she would tell you the details of our private correspondence."

"Correspondence." I let out a breath. "That's a pretty fancy term for sabotage. Betrayal. Need I go on?"

"I'd prefer that you didn't."

"And for your information, Charlotte didn't show me the e-mails. I looked at her laptop when she left the room. Yes, I was devious and under-handed. I learned from the best, after all."

Anger flashes across his golden eyes. "That information is confidential."

"My body is confidential, you asshole."

He cocks his head. "The pictures. You saw them."

It takes everything in me not to launch myself at him, to use my broken nails like claws, to bite him. He makes me savage, like the wild animal that he is. "Yes, the pictures. The pictures you took. The pictures you shared. Did that make you feel better about what my father did? Ruining him wasn't enough? Deflowering me wasn't enough?"

"Stop," he says roughly. "I didn't share any pictures of you."

"I saw them!"

"Then you know they don't match the photos we took in this room. You never took off your panties, your bra. Your face was hidden by your hair."

My teeth clench so hard I hear grinding. "I know what pictures we took."

"And I sure as hell didn't share them, even

though I had a right to. Damon gave me hell for not passing them on, but I wasn't letting anyone see what was mine."

"Yours? Oh no, I don't belong to you. Not then, not now."

"I have a winning bid on an auction that says otherwise. The thirty days aren't up yet."

"That can't come fast enough," I say, challenging him. I've never been this fearless confronting him, facing anyone, but he's pushed me to the edge. "And I already know those pictures didn't come from this room, but you could have taken them anytime I was in your house."

An electric silence fills the space around us, setting the colored light in the room on edge. Blue and yellow dust motes dance around us, energized.

"You think—" His nostrils flare. "You think I took pictures of you while you were in my house, without you knowing?"

"How else does someone have them?"

He continues as if I didn't speak, working it through with slow, pained deliberation. "And you think I shared those pictures with the world out of spite, out of revenge on a girl who's done nothing wrong."

Doubt flickers inside me. "Didn't you?"

I expect him to admit it—he's never shied away from what he's done. If anything he seems to take perverse pleasure in threatening me, in using me, in pointing out all the ways he hurts me.

Or maybe he'll deny it, after all. He'll defend his honor with the same vigor and violence with which he went after my father. He'll come after me, and when we clash, it will be so satisfying.

He does neither of those things. Instead he stalks to the window, large hands cradling the window frame, large body canting forward. Over his shoulder I can see the city's skyline rising high and swerving sideways, like looking through a fun-house mirror.

"You have good reason to suspect me," he says softly.

I take a step closer. "Don't."

"I'm sorry, Avery." But it's not the kind of apology that comes with an admission. It's soft and thoughtful, the kind that would come from a man who gives a shit about me.

"Don't pull this reverse psychology bullshit on me. I know what you did."

A short laugh, without any humor. "And what are you going to do about it, little virgin? You're powerless. No money. No one to help you. Living one step up from a cardboard box."

It stings to hear him lay it out so plainly, but I have the feeling it hurts him too.

"I can fight back," I warn him. I'm still pumped enough to do it, finally pushed beyond all sanity. I could hit him, kick him. Bite him. Even with the unspooling thread of doubt that he did this to me, I'd be able to hurt someone for the first time in my life.

"Like you did in the attic?" He turns to face me. "I won't stop you this time."

And I realize this is my own personal Rubicon, the line I'm going to cross. There will be two versions of Avery James, the one who was a victim and the one who's a warrior. The one who refused to do harm and the one who slaps a man who won't defend himself. I'm not sure which version of me is better, but I'm hurting enough to do it anyway. All I have to do is remember the grainy black-and-white pictures of me, taken when I didn't know it. Shared to humiliate and shame me. All I have to do is remember Justin saying he forgives me for something I didn't even do.

"Go ahead," he murmurs. "I didn't take those pictures, but I'm not going to pretend I'm innocent. If I hadn't ruined your father, he wouldn't have turned on his partners. They wouldn't have attacked him. You'd have a protector in the world instead of being alone."

My hands clench into fists. "Keep going."

His eyes flash with something—maybe regret. Maybe relief. "And that business deal where your father cheated me? Even before that it wasn't completely legal. He was desperate enough to sell his business for more than it was worth. Desperate enough to include you in the package."

"No," I whisper. What does that even mean—*include you?* Like I'm an object, a little yellow price tag stamped on my breast. "You're lying."

"One month."

"He would never have asked me that."

"Of course not. He would have arranged for you to find out about his debts. Maybe your credit card would get declined when you tried to buy notebooks and pencils. And then he'd break down and confess how dire the situation was, how horrible I am. If only there was something he could do to please me, something he could give me—"

"No." My voice rises to a shout. "No. No."

"I already bought your virginity, Avery. You've always been mine."

Grief and rage collide in a toxic miasma, blurring my vision. A keening sound fills the air, and I realize it's me. And then I'm doing it; I'm hitting him, again and again, his cheek red with the blows. I'm using all my strength and it barely moves him, the *smack* ugly and loud. It's the sound of someone breaking—but not him. It's me.

When he finally catches me in his arms, I'm sobbing, incoherent.

"Shh," he says. "You have to stop. You'll hurt yourself."

When he says it, I realize that my hand is throbbing. That's how strong he is, how impenetrable. Like beating myself against a brick wall. He'll still be standing in a hundred years.

"No," I say, voice thick with tears. "You're lying. You're lying."

Except he's not. I know because he promised to tell me the truth. And he's kept his word time and time again. It feels like losing a part of me, a limb torn off, to hear what Daddy did. How could he do it? Some truths you'd rather not hear.

His hands move over me, soothing, tender. "I know, sweetheart. I know."

"She didn't love him," I say, voice still broken by tears.

"I know."

I don't ask how he does, but that's true too. There are secrets in my family. Secrets so dark I'm beginning to wonder if they buried my mother deeper than the drunk driver ever did. There's only been one constant. Gabriel Miller. That he's wanted me. He's taken me. *You've always been mine.*

His hands frame my face. I must look terrible with my eyes red from crying, grief staining my face, but the reverence in his gaze leaves no doubt what he sees. Someone beautiful.

"Listen to me," he says softly. "Your mother lived in a time when women didn't have many choices. She did the best she could for her family. She was strong—damn near invincible."

I never doubted my mother. "Why are you telling me this?"

His thumbs sweep away my tears. "Because that's what you did. That's what you are."

"I don't live in her time."

"Don't you? Your father wanted to keep you his little girl. He would let you out of your room for parties to impress the other grownups with how smart you are. Justin wanted a trophy, something to parade around and lord over the other frat boys."

"And you?"

"I'm the worst of them," he says softly. "I want to own every inch of your skin, to be the only man who touches you, who tastes you. You think I wouldn't bid on a woman? That I shouldn't bid on you, of all people? I'll spend every cent I have, break every goddamn law to keep you."

A shiver runs through me. "You wanted the auction."

"Wanted it? No. Those were the worst hours of my life, knowing that other men would see you. That they might touch you. I wanted to smash their faces in, every single one of them."

"Then why did you suggest it?"

"Would you have sold yourself to me if I had suggested it at the Den?"

"No."

"And what about if your father had come to you, told you to sleep with me in order to pay his debts?"

I swallow hard. "I don't know."

"Oh, I think you would have. I think you'd have done anything for your precious daddy, but he got cold feet. After the ink dried, when he went home and looked into your eyes, he didn't want to go through with it."

It's hard to take comfort in that, knowing he

agreed to the deal in the first place. "And no one backs out of a deal with you."

"For that alone I would have ruined him, but I wanted you. He should have known I'd have you no matter what. Whether he agreed or not. Whether you wanted me or not."

"Why are you telling me now?"

His lips twist in cold amusement. "I didn't count on how well you could play the game."

"I lost everything."

"It wasn't a fair trade," he admits softly. "My black heart for everything you hold dear. Your only solace is that I'm ruined even worse. An empty shell."

"What are you saying?" I whisper.

"Do you remember when I told you to kneel?"

My heart thuds. "I can't forget."

"Why did you do it?"

"Because I wanted the diary." Except that's not the whole truth. And doesn't he deserve that? I wanted him broken, bleeding, and he's doing that. This proud man admitting defeat. "And because I wanted you."

His eyes burn like the sun, painful and bright. "Do you know what it did to me? God, I was so ready to take you. I would have taken you and taken you. Never giving anything back. Understand? I never thought for one second that you'd give yourself to me willingly."

"You never came to me."

"I never believed I could have you without buying you," he says, his voice flat.

There's nothing in his tone to reveal emotion, no hint of weakness. How long did it take him to perfect that facade? How much power does it require to maintain those walls? I know the truth about him—about Gabriel's father and his moonshine. His whorehouse. What did Gabriel Miller see that made him think he wasn't worthy of love?

"Kneel," I say softly.

He stills. "Repeat that."

It's a dangerous game, making a lion bow in front of you. One I'm willing to play if it means winning. It's not only my safety that's at stake, but my heart. Not as black as Gabriel's, but more fragile. "Kneel."

In the heartbeats that follow, he could storm from the room. He could push me down on the floor and have his way with me. There are a million outcomes besides what he does. One knee on the floor. Then the other. With his height and breadth, he still comes to my chest.

This is the part where he tucked my head against his thigh, where he absolved me in a wordless balm. Where I could feel his arousal, already hard and throbbing.

His hands go to my jeans, careful and sure.

It's like a fever, an intense burn that makes my skin warm and pink, that makes me shudder. His fingers are blunt as they stroke down my stomach, into the slick crest between my legs.

"Fuck," he breathes.

And then he fuses his lips to my clit, making me buck in surprise. I knew what he wanted from me, but the slide of his tongue is still a shock. I cry out, and he groans his approval.

He pulls back to meet my eyes. "That's right. Let them hear you. They'll never get to taste you like this. Never get to feel your clit against their lips, will they?"

"Oh God," I gasp. "No, no."

Male satisfaction makes his eyes glow. "This pretty little cunt has always been mine. Say it."

Those words. My cheeks flush. "This pretty—"

Two fingers nudge at my opening, pressing inside with a possessive force. My flesh molds around him, clenching and clenching, trying to pull him deeper. "Finish."

"This pretty little—"

He leans forward to work a slow lick from his fingers to my clit, the extended contact a blissful agony. My hips rock against him, begging, desperate.

I know what he wants. "This pretty little cunt has always…"

When he sucks my clit, I lose all sense of time and space. I'm floating in a sea of sunlight and pleasure, only his mouth and his fingers and the rough sound of his encouragement.

He holds me on the brink until tears leak down my cheeks. It hurts, and I whimper. He's merciless, teasing me with gentle licks and twists of his fingers.

"Always yours," I manage to gasp. "I've always been yours."

His fingers curl inside me, and I rise up on my toes. The pleasure radiates from my core, blooming over my breasts, my lips, all the way down to my toes. My mouth opens on a silent cry. His teeth graze my clit, and then I scream. They all hear me—those men downstairs. The dangerous ones, the powerful ones. They know who owns me now. And I know too.

Chapter Twenty-Five

AFTER THE ORGASM hits, my legs crumple beneath me. Gabriel catches me in his lap, cradling me as pleasure renders me helpless. The tidal wave of pleasure recedes, but the water remains, lapping at my skin in remembered relief.

Gabriel doesn't hold anything back, murmuring soft words while he strokes my hair. This is a side of him I haven't seen before, but one I always knew existed—the natural counterpoint to his strictly enforced stoicism. He was so careful never to be kind, so deliberate in his remoteness. And God maybe that was for the best, because his tenderness hits me harder than the orgasm. A few seconds and I'm already addicted. *You were always mine.*

He moves before I'm ready, fixing my clothes and leading me downstairs.

Damon Scott waits for us, wearing a forbidding expression.

Through the link of our hands, I feel Gabriel

tense. "We're leaving."

"Don't you think you've done enough?" Damon asks.

The temperature drops by twenty degrees. "Clearly I don't, since I'm taking her home with me. Since when are you the police around here?"

"Since I found out I failed her."

The question strikes a chord in me—curiosity mingled with expectation. Something is happening, pieces moving into place around me. Not quite understanding the choices of my opponent but trusting that they have meaning. Which means the final blow is coming.

Exhaustion weighs down my limbs, my eyelids. The shock of my father's involvement in my downfall, the blissful respite that Gabriel's mouth offered. They lay a blanket over me, shielding me from the world.

"You have nothing to do with this," Gabriel says, voice tight.

"I think I do. I'm the one who sold her to you. My—"

"No, Damon. She's mine. And I don't think you want to get between me and what's mine. You aren't suicidal."

The threat is delivered with cold certainty, between two men who are friends. I don't want to get between them. My family's secrets are a dark vine, winding its way through the city, thorns leaving marks everywhere it goes.

"Please," I whisper. "Don't fight."

The ticking of the grandfather clock marks the tension in inexorable evenness.

Damon studies me, dark gaze impersonal but thorough as it takes in my weariness. "There's a week left of the thirty days, but I don't give a fuck about that. Not anymore. Do you want to go with him?"

Gabriel's hand tightens on mine. Clearly he's willing to fight his way through, fight his friend. My heart has been cracked and battered ever since the auction, but the final blow is this—realizing that Gabriel still thinks I'll say no. That he has to buy me, to force me, that I could never want him on my own.

"I want to go," I say, my voice clear.

Damon's expression reveals he still doubts the truth of it, but he doesn't stand in our way. I don't know what change of heart made him auction me, as emotionless as if I were a Persian rug, and then suddenly decide to help me. But I don't need his help. Not about this.

Without another word Gabriel leads me past Damon, down the hallway and out the front door. A black limo waits in the damp air, raindrops glittering on the glossy tinted windows. Then we're pulling away from the Den, heading toward Gabriel's home, side by side in the deep shadowy interior.

A shiver works through me, and Gabriel changes the settings to warm me. I feel hot air blowing on me, but it can't touch the coldness inside me. Only Gabriel's hands do that, his body as he curves around me, his lips as he murmurs against my temple.

"Thank you," he says.

"It's coming apart," I whisper.

"What is?"

The carefully constructed tangle of lies my father has built. And I'm afraid to see what thread appears next. Afraid to find out the rest of my mother's story. "Did he really sell me?"

"I'm sorry, Avery."

Pain can't touch me now. Grief. Fear. "Keep me," I say softly. "The rest of the thirty days. Don't send me away again."

His arms tighten around me. "I won't."

"The pictures."

"I'll find out who took them. Who vandalized the house." Gabriel's voice is grim. "He'll wish he hadn't."

My eyes close against the possibilities. "I don't understand. Why now?"

"I had security on the house. When you came to get your photos taken, you mentioned someone had been at your house at night."

Old terror tightens my chest. "I convinced myself I had imagined that."

"That would have been the best-case scenario, but I put security on the house anyway. Even after you were with me."

"Because Daddy was still there." And I realize that part of the weariness I saw in his eyes was from my father's injuries. "And you didn't pay for his care just because of me."

"Some people think the point of chess is to kill the king. You know the truth."

"*Checkmate.* It comes from the Persian verb for *to remain.* It means he's helpless. Trapped." My lashes lower. "Is that what you wanted to do to my father?"

"It's the ultimate victory. Not that he should die, be made a martyr, mourned by a daughter he doesn't deserve. I want him trapped in every sense of the word, unable to make another move, but alive and fully aware of his loss."

"That's disturbing."

"That's chess."

Realization dawns. "And you stopped security after the auction, after I lost the house and you were no longer responsible for it."

"Yes."

"And that's when someone vandalized it." Someone who had pictures of me naked. Possibly the same person who had tried to break into my house while I was home. "But why didn't they come after me directly?"

"They probably figured you'd find out what happened at the house."

"But the motel would have been so much easier to break into." I draw in a sharp breath. "You had security there too, didn't you?"

"Not as much as I wanted, but some. And I made it known that you were under my protection. No one would have gotten into your room, that was for damn sure."

It clicks, then. "Will. You put him there."

"We had an understanding."

Questions flood my mind. Did Will tell him everything that had happened, including Justin spending part of the night? Did he call Gabriel the night we got high? Is that why he came to check on me? Maybe another girl would have found that kind of watchfulness unnerving, but right now I find comfort in it. In a world where men would control me, Gabriel protects me.

It's not the same thing as freedom.

My mother settled for safety, too. Maybe that can be enough.

CHAPTER TWENTY-SIX

I WAKE UP with moonlight across my face. I'm wearing a T-shirt and panties, the sheet tangled around my legs. I thought he would send me to my room, like before, but instead he carried me to his bed. Exhausted, worn down, I fell asleep.

Gabriel lies next to me, his powerful body in rare repose. He doesn't look young in sleep, only softer. Without the strict control he maintains while awake.

Lashes against his cheeks, incongruous fragility on a body compact with muscle. A shadow darkens his jaw. My legs move restlessly as I remember the burn of his bristle between them.

A sprinkling of wiry hair covers his chest and narrows, angling down. The sheet crosses his abs, and I use two careful fingers to move it aside. Cotton briefs mold to his body, revealing narrow hips and the shape of his cock against his thigh, large even in sleep. I still remember the taste of him, the salt and musk. Beneath the sheet his legs almost reach the base of the bed, making even the oversize frame look miniature.

"Enjoying yourself," comes his husky voice.

My gaze snaps to his. Embarrassment wipes all the words from my brain.

He laughs, his lids low with sleep. "Don't stop, little virgin. I think I can come from you looking at me."

Of course I can't bear to look at him now—can't look at his body, can't even meet his eyes. "You're mocking me."

"God, you have no idea what you do to me." He takes my hand, guiding it over his briefs.

Hot. Hard. Throbbing. "Oh," comes out as a squeak.

His voice roughens. "Stroke it."

I run my fingers lightly over his length, feeling him through the fabric. A damp spot stains the tip, and I press my forefinger there, making him grunt. A small smile touches my lips. He's right that there's power here, power in making him shift on the bed, his body so strong, made vulnerable by my touch.

"You like this," I say softly, shyly.

His voice leaves no doubt. "I crave it."

My gaze trails back over his body, snagging on the nightstand.

And there's the pawn piece, the dark trophy that I had feared. My breath catches. I look away, not wanting him to see my pain. This is the bed where he took my virginity. These are the sheets that had been stained with my blood—bleached white now.

"Hey." He grasps my chin and turns me to face him. "Talk to me."

"The pawn."

He follows my gaze, understanding hitting his light brown eyes. "I won't hurt you again. The first time—"

"It wasn't painful like that." I close my eyes tight. "Well, it was, but that's not what hurt the most. It was how you pushed me away after, like that's all I'm good for."

His eyes go dark, more bronze now. "You think I only want you for sex?"

"You paid for me, Gabriel. That's not something a man does if he wants a relationship."

"I don't want a relationship," he says roughly. "I want to own you."

"You don't mean that."

"Your family has dark secrets. Well, this is mine. That my father owned women—not just because it made him money. Not just so he could fuck them. He bought and sold them because that's what he wanted to do, that was the only thing that got him off."

My chest constricts. "And that's what you want to do—sell me?"

"Never." A cold laugh. "I'm too fucking possessive for that. No one else gets to touch you."

"What if you get tired of me?"

"I tried, little virgin. I sent you away. I tried to forget you, but I get hard just looking at a chess piece. I can't seem to let you go." A rough sound. "A lifetime of discipline and now I'm a fucking addict."

I bite my lip. "What if I get tired of you?"

He growls, flipping me over in a whirl of male strength. I'm face-first against the bed, his body framing mine. He nuzzles the base of my neck, a primal show of possession. "Mine," he whispers.

I fought that word before. I resented it even as I hated it.

Now my secret muscles clench in tacit acquiescence.

His knee nudges my legs apart. He pushes my hair aside, fingers clenching in the strands. A hot press of his mouth against my back, following down my spine until I'm spread apart and wanting.

Blunt fingers force their way inside me, finding me wet. He groans in approval. "Fuck yes."

Even his fingers feel thick in the small space, my skin struggling to adjust around him. His cock is even bigger. He twists his fingers, seeking a spot, finding it—and I arch against the bed, wordless sounds begging for release.

When he took my virginity, I faced him. It had seemed like a powerless position, the depth and speed of the thrusts completely his to command. Submission in the most base animal language. But I realize now the range of motion that I had to touch him, to wrap my legs around him, to press my breasts against his chest. Now I'm entirely motionless, his hand in my hair holding me above, his weight holding me down from behind. I can't touch him.

"Please," I whisper. "I need… I need…"

He gives me a little shake with a fistful of my hair. "You take what I give you."

I groan my dissent, without even leverage to push back against him. His cock burns a slick trail across my butt as he presses a kiss to my cheek. Only a second later do I realize that kiss was a warning, maybe even an apology. The wide head of his cock nudges against my folds. Without a word he thrusts inside me, ripping past clenched muscles, forcing me open. A pained cry is muffled by the sheets. My body reacts instinctively, inching up the bed in a frantic bid to escape. It only succeeds in tightening the pull on my scalp.

A calloused hand angles my hips, and then he plunges again, thudding against a point inside me. My mouth opens on a silent scream. His entire body covers mine, chest against my back, hips covering mine, arm stretching out along mine and grasping my wrist. My hands clench and open, desperate for some mooring. There's nothing but his body in a sea of wild sensation, every rock of his body bursting stars behind my eyelids. Orgasm crashes through me, violent and stormy, never-ending as I contract and pulse and quiver around him.

It's too much, this relentless throb inside me, this powerful bass he makes with my body. I can't breathe, can't speak. This is what he meant when he said he owns me—the complete capture of my body, the takeover of my mind. I'm drowning in Gabriel Miller, the scent and sound of him. The feel of him inside me.

"So good," he says, dark and almost angry. "So fucking good."

I feel when he breaks, the stark sound of loss he makes, the fail of his rhythm, the way he holds me to him instead of holding me down. His body empties into me—his come, his despair. His desperate weakness for a woman he shouldn't want.

CHAPTER TWENTY-SEVEN

THE NEXT DAY when I wake up, Gabriel is gone, but there's a phone on the bedside table. I know it's meant for me because the pawn sits on top of it. When I turn it on, there are three numbers already saved—Harper's cell phone, the number to Mr. Stewart in the nursing home.

The last number says *Asshole.*

He answers after the first ring. "Good morning."

"Where are you?"

"Downstairs. I have a few things to take care of in my office, but I'll be done in time for lunch."

"Am I allowed to wander?" There's a hint of snark in my voice, but it's also a serious question. I don't know what the rules are for this new tenuous truce.

"Of course," he says. "Just don't get lost."

His house is ridiculous with hallways that lead in circles, with bedrooms that lead into deeper rooms. I don't know whether he bought it this way or had it built, but it suits him. "I thought you like the chase."

A low laugh. "Don't tease me, little virgin. I have all afternoon to make you regret it."

I shiver, knowing he can accomplish it. My body still aches with all the ways he took me last night, waking me over and over, sometimes moving inside me before I was awake, time folding on itself. "Do I get clothes?"

"In the dresser. Top drawer."

Crossing the room, I find the contents of my motel room neatly stacked. I nudge aside my clothes, a few books. "The chess set is missing."

"In the library," he says, voice velvet with promise. "I thought we might play."

"Said the spider to the fly."

He doesn't deny it. "I'm looking forward to it."

My fingers brush against the bottom of the drawer. That's it. "Wait. Where's the diary?"

"We still have a week left."

The final week he won in the auction. "What does that have to do with this?"

"You can have it back when we're done. Unless you find it on your own."

Red flashes across my vision. "Why do you

play games?"

"Why do you assume it's a game?"

"Because you have no reason to keep it from me."

"So you say."

I close my eyes, taking a deep breath. Does it matter? In the large scheme of things I've gone years without reading the diary. I can go a few more days. "One week."

And like we're signing a treaty: "One week."

What will happen after that? Will he send me away or ask me to stay?

Is he even capable of asking something? All he knows how to do is purchase me. Once the escrow transfers to me, I won't be for sale anymore—I won't need money. I won't need Gabriel.

After hanging up, I call Harper. She tells me that she returned to New York City with Christopher, that they're locked in some kind of battle, neither willing to give in.

She's fuming. "He's doing this just to piss me off."

"I know the feeling," I say drily. "Except…"

"Except what?" she snaps, her voice rich with warning.

"As your friend I want the best for you. I want

you to be happy."

She sighs. "This is one of those tough love situations, isn't it?"

"I'm just saying it seems like he's trying to do right by you. And it kind of feels…" I clear my throat. "I mean, is it possible you're spending more just to make him angry?"

"It's my money!"

"Right, but he was tasked with managing your money."

"My money, not managing *me*. He's ridiculous. And horrible. And did I mention ridiculous?"

"Well, sure. Yes. But you know he takes his job seriously. It was in your dad's will. It's not like he can question what exactly the man's intentions were. He looked up to your dad. He wouldn't want to fail him in his last request."

"Stop being reasonable," she huffs. "He's horrible."

"Horrible," I agree.

"I can't believe you're siding with him after what Landon Moore did to you. He trashed your trust fund! You lost your house because of him! He should be behind bars. He's the one who should be bedridden. I'd kick his ass for you. If, you know, I weren't five foot nothing."

"I appreciate that, but Landon stole from me. You don't think Christopher's messing with your money, do you?"

She sounds more aggrieved than ever. "No, he actually made it bigger with his investments. And don't you dare say that's a good thing. Chicks before dicks. We agreed."

"I'm pretty sure I never agreed to that, much less heard you say it. But for what it's worth, I'd kick his ass for you. If, you know, I wasn't stuck being the not-quite-virginal sex slave of a rich asshole."

The asshole and I live the next few days in a sex dream, never leaving the house, barely leaving his large four-post bed. There's an urgency to our lovemaking, an unspoken awareness that the end is near.

In the mornings he works from his office, and I explore the house—searching for the diary. It's a half-hearted search, fueled more by curiosity than any real desire to end this. Because the end is coming soon enough. I don't need to hurry it along.

The gaps in my knowledge loom outside these four walls, waiting, watching. They'll find me soon enough, but for now I'm safe in Gabriel's arms.

Chapter Twenty-Eight

B Y THE LAST day I'm certain I've looked everywhere for the diary. It still eludes me. I even checked outside the house, almost getting lost amid the tall hedges shaped into an elaborate maze. I'm actually more impressed that Justin made it through that during my last stay.

I wake when the moon is high, suddenly alert. Did I hear something? Or is it only my anxiety, wondering what tomorrow will bring? This might be my last night in this bed. I know that Gabriel cares about me, but I'm not sure he's capable of having a regular relationship. Not sure he wants to try.

On a whim I pick up the pawn from the side table.

Slipping from the bed, I walk barefoot through the empty halls. The air still smells faintly of the fresh biscuits Mrs. B. made for dinner. I turn sideways into the library, the fireplace dark in the middle of the night. There's a small lamp on the table with the chess set.

I put the pawn in its place.

We never did play, not with the set, but we played our own version—the instinctive waters of middlegame. Openings are strategic, mapped out and named. Analyzed with strengths and weaknesses. But middlegames contain infinite combinations, too complex to define. Both fighting for control of the board, trading with the fervent hope that we'll come out on top.

Keeping the king in relative safety, because that's the point of the game.

My fingertip touches each piece on the black side—king, queen. Knight.

An unusual piece because of the way it moves. Forward and sideways. The only piece able to jump other pieces. Not the most powerful on the board, but the most dangerous in closed positions.

I pick up the king, my thumb stroking over the ridges, the cross at the top.

Once I read that Napoleon Bonaparte loved chess, though he hadn't been an extraordinary player. He had played his generals, certain the game held some kind of tactical education. He played every day of his exile, though I don't remember who he played with. His guards? That hits a little close to home.

And I remember something else—that an escape plan was hatched to hide instructions in a chess piece and send it to him as a gift. The piece in my hand is too small to hide anything, at least anything readable to the naked eye. But the base of the set is tall. Gabriel had it custom carved for my arrival.

I set down the king and test the set, careful not to knock over the lined-up pieces. Heavy. Some sets come with hollow compartments to store the pieces, but this one feels solid.

Unless there's something inside.

Tipping the surface, I let the pieces slide onto the rug. The king rolls onto the hardwood near the fireplace. I lift the lid of the chessboard and look inside—a leather-bound book sits in the empty space.

My mother's diary.

I should be happy to have found it, even a day sooner than he had promised to give it back. Instead all I feel is dread. All the demons we've been keeping at bay—they're free now. Free in the form of beautiful scrolling handwriting and a lifetime of secrets.

Turning the pages past wedding plans and honeymoon, past her excited and elaborate plans for the house that Daddy builds her, a single word catches my eye.

Afraid.

My hand trembles as I flip back to find the page.

Everything I wanted has come true—a beautiful house. A kind husband. Security for my family. And yet I can't shake the feeling that I made a terrible mistake. Even in my own room I can feel someone watching me, threatening me. I'm afraid that I'm going insane.

Was my mother insane? It sounds like paranoia. Diagnoses and treatment of mental illness wasn't like today. They had less knowledge and far more stigma.

I remember feeling like someone watched me.

Maybe I'm going insane too.

Except someone had written *WHORE* over the fireplace. That's not a figment of my imagination, an illness that needs to be treated. And someone took pictures of me.

Geoffrey insists that it's in my head, but I'm sure it's not. It's like the house is alive. Breathing. Whispering. I'm never alone, even when the people have gone.

Unease moves through me. I glance at the shadows around me. I can't see through them, but I know I'm alone. Don't I? I remember my terror the night I saw someone outside the window. Is that how my mother felt all the time?

I thought she loved the house. And at the beginning she did.

It turned into something sinister in these pages.

The strangest thing happened tonight. I saw Jonathan at a party for the Alberts' anniversary. We both pretended we had never met. When he asked me to dance, I said yes so we could talk. I asked him how he got an invitation. He told me he had worked with Ralph Albert, but he refused to go into details.

So the mystery man had a name. Jonathan. Not that it told me anything. I didn't know anyone by that name, and it's common enough that it wouldn't help me if I did.

But Geoffrey acted strange the rest of the night. He kept asking me about my dance with Jonathan, even though we had maintained appearances. It's almost as if he knows the truth.

He did, because he had followed my mother the night before their wedding.

Now I'm wondering if the eyes I feel inside the house have a name. Geoffrey James.

"Ah, you found it."

The voice startles me, and I jump from the chair. The diary falls to the rug amid the scattered chess pieces. This is the way he found me weeks ago, at the beginning of our month. Now we're here at the end. I know him better, but there are even more questions.

Gabriel isn't wearing a shirt, just low-slung slacks that reveal muscled abs and a trail of dark hair. He looks unrepentant about hiding the diary, about having startled me, but then he always did like to play.

CHAPTER TWENTY-NINE

GABRIEL CROSSES THE room to the fireplace, kneeling to reveal the bunched muscles of his back. He settles a stack of logs from the metal basket beside the fireplace and strikes a match. The roar fills the vacuum of quiet with crackles and pops of a new fire. When he faces me, the light flickers against his broad shoulders, his muscled arms, leaving his expression an enigma.

I pick up the diary with two fingers, as if it's poison. And God, it is. How long has it been poisoning that house? How long has it been making me sick without even knowing it? And Gabriel doesn't seem the least bit surprised.

"How did you know my mother was afraid?"

He settles into the other armchair, long legs stretched out. He's the king of his domain—and a checkmate against him seems nearly impossible. How had I ever thought I could make him helpless? Abandoned? "Because she told someone," he says.

"Who?"

"The father of my good friend Damon Scott." His tone is sardonic. "You may remember him."

I swallow my shock. "Hard to forget the man who auctioned my virginity."

"His father, Jonathan Scott. That's who she was going to see the night she was murdered."

The night she was murdered…when she was still married to my father. When she wore rubies and a beautiful dress. *Stay home, sweetheart. Stay small. That's when you're safe.*

Stay safe.

"She didn't have an affair," I say, not quite believing it.

"I didn't say that. Only that she didn't feel safe. She told her old lover. He promised to protect her, and on the night she planned to leave Geoffrey James, she died."

Cold doubt slices through me. "You think it was my father. That he killed her."

"It's more important what you think."

"You're just saying that so I'll abandon him. The ultimate victory, that's what you called it." And if I turn away from my father, he will have truly lost. "He couldn't have been the one lurking outside the house at night. He wasn't the one who vandalized my house."

"If you say so," Gabriel says, sounding uncon-cerned.

"He wouldn't have hurt her. He loved her." Except I remember the way he'd talked about her flaws, with the horrible acceptance. As if he could have blamed her.

"You say that as if it's a good thing. Love. In my experience it makes everything worse. It makes people do horrible things, things they'd never commit otherwise."

He isn't talking about my parents anymore.

He's talking about himself. "What are you so afraid of?"

"Afraid? No. I think fear is a more rational feeling. Like hunger. Desire. Natural expressions of the human condition."

"So is love."

"No, love is a game. Like chess. One you're going to lose."

I don't have anything left—not if I doubt my own father, my only family. Not if I'm afraid of the walls around me. "Like my mother lost?"

"Did she?"

"You know what happened to her."

"I really don't."

The answer has been hovering at the edge of my consciousness for a long time—before I found the diary. Before Gabriel ruined my father. Maybe from the beginning, when I huddled under my covers as a child.

"Someone killed her. It wasn't a drunk driving accident. That's what Daddy didn't want me to find. That's what you didn't want me to find either. Everyone's trying to keep me in the dark. Why? Why can't I know that she was murdered? Who are you protecting?"

"The only person I'm trying to protect is you."

The words ring with truth, but I don't know if I can believe him. This might be part of his plan. To make me turn away from my father. To break the final bond of the James family.

"It hurts me more to keep secrets. That's the legacy of my family more than anything. Lies. Half-truths. Smiles that hide more than they share. I'm sick of it. Tell me, Gabriel. If you care about me at all, tell me."

He looks away. "If I tell you, you'll have no reason to stay."

"Then love me enough to let me leave."

A rough laugh. "And you still think love isn't a game."

He stands, the glint in his eye threatening to prove his point. And God help me, but I want him to try. If this is all he can offer me, then I want him to play.

With a sweep of his arm he moves the chess pieces.

He pulls me down on the rug, the pile like velvet against my palms. He presses a kiss to my forehead, almost innocent except for the hard length I feel against my thigh. One kiss on each of my eyelids. I suck in a breath at the tenderness in his lips. His mouth moves down my jaw, warm presses that leave a trail of fire. He reaches my neck, and I arch my body to give him access.

Between the valley of my breasts.

"Wait," I gasp.

My legs press together, but his knee is already between them. He moves inexorably lower, pushing up my nightgown, pressing open-mouthed kisses across my stomach, the flick of his tongue a promise of what's to come.

His hands pull aside the placket of my panties.

A long lick through my center makes me cry out. "Wait, wait, wait."

He lifts his head to send me a half smile, pure masculine revenge. "Wait for what?"

"It's just so much, and I need to catch my breath." I'm rambling, but I can't seem to stop. "And I don't know if this is the right place to do—"

His finger stroking down my cleft tightens my throat. Only a strangled sound emerges.

His lids lower. "Time's up, beautiful."

The rug that had felt soft a moment ago now feels like a bed of nails, my skin impossibly sensitive. And the touch of his tongue to my clit is pure torture, a sharp ache that runs the length of my body. I writhe on the floor, unsure if I want to get away or seek more.

Something brushes my fingers, and I clasp it. Small. Cool.

A pawn. The same one he once used on my body? Maybe. It's anonymous now, as smooth and shiny as every other pawn. Indistinguishable.

He sees what I'm holding, his eyes flickering with brutal amusement.

A queen on the floor catches his eye. He picks it up, considering.

"No," I say, not wanting the sharp curves of her crown anywhere near my sensitive places.

He laughs and sets it on my stomach instead, just above my belly button. I breathe nice and slow, moving the piece in a gentle wave. He adds a bishop. A rook.

"They're going to fall," I warn him, holding in a breathless laugh. My stomach is flat enough to hold the pieces, but not if I move around, not if I breathe too hard. Definitely not if I orgasm.

"Then you'd better be careful," he warns, adding another pawn. "If they fall down, I'm going to stop."

"I can't," I breathe, more panicked now than when I told him to wait.

His mouth descends on me, and any tenderness is gone. He's relentless with lips and teeth and tongue, moving through my folds, licking at my clit, until my whole body feels taut as a wire. "Please, please, please."

No answer. He doesn't even pause, his mouth working at a merciless game.

The chess pieces tremble along with my body, wobbling from side to side on my stomach even as I struggle to control my breathing. I'm too close, and the panting knocks the queen to the ground.

He pulls away, his lips still damp with my arousal. "Too bad."

"Don't stop," I say, and like dominoes the other pieces topple to the ground.

A low chuckle. "You should have stayed still, little virgin."

He can't leave me like this. "I need you," I whimper.

"Fuck," he breathes. "I can't say no to you."

I press my hips into the air, silently begging, beyond words now.

He answers by opening his pants. I don't see him from here, only feel him in blind need, the blunt press of him, the hot stretch. And then his body covers mine, a full thrust that has me crying out into the tall library, the sound captured by the hundreds of books, thousands, their leather spines and old pages, holding my pleasure and pain for eternity.

The silk of my nightgown chafes, driving my arousal even higher.

His mouth touches mine, tongue nudging my lips apart. In his kiss I taste myself, salt and a feminine musk. I taste the need and pent-up fury that he's been hiding. He can put the chess pieces up like a wall between us, but when it comes down, I see him clearly, feel every hungry thrust inside me, hear every rough grunt he makes on entry, live in every heartbeat that he looks into my eyes, walls torn down for a few priceless moments as the climax hits us both.

Chapter Thirty

ONLY AFTER HE pulls out, after we've had sex, does he undress me and himself completely. It's a new kind of intimacy to be naked when we're both sated, bare in every sense of the word.

"You're beautiful," he murmurs, running his hand over my hip.

Our bodies are a study in contrasts, mine pale and smooth, his made of scars. I copy the motion over him, feeling something small and puckered at his back. I sit up, peeking over his body.

"What happened here?"

"Bullet," he says casually.

"You were shot? With a gun?"

"That's typically where bullets come from."

"Don't make jokes. That's horrible. What happened?"

"A customer didn't want to pay. Or didn't I mention that? I worked as an enforcer for my father. When a bastard wanted to fuck a girl and then leave without paying."

"The brothel."

"The brothel," he says, voice carefree, but I feel the tension in his body. Muscles hard, pulse beating faster. "That's a nice word for the dirty old building where men hurt women."

I swallow hard. What kind of initiation into sex did he have? Mine was unconventional, no doubt. The auction itself had been humiliating. But Gabriel had always been gentle with my body. He showed me pleasure from the very first time.

"How did you lose your virginity?"

A cruel smile. "How do you think? With one of the girls, of course."

"You paid her?"

"No, that was a gift from dear old dad. I only found that out after the fact. A fourteen-year-old boy doesn't ask many question when a beautiful woman shows him her tits. Which is a fucking shame."

"Did anyone…" I force the words out quick-ly. "Did anyone hurt you?"

He's silent a moment. "Not like you mean. My father insisted I work for him, but not with sex. With fists. Knives. Guns. If someone didn't want to pay, it was my job to convince them."

"That's horrible."

"I was damn good at it. Business was never

better."

"Oh, Gabriel."

"Don't look at me with pity," he says with a harsh laugh. "It was my job to keep the girls in line, too. If one of them mouthed off to a customer or wouldn't do what they wanted, I had to show them the light."

I'm afraid to ask, but I have to know. It comes as a whisper, hesitant. "How?"

Our gazes meet. "I hurt them."

Something in my heart cracks. "No."

"Yes," he says forcefully. "I held their wrists too hard, looked into their eyes, and promised to bury their bodies if they didn't do what we told them."

Tears stream down my cheeks. I don't want to think I had illusions about Gabriel Miller, but I know that I must have. Because they're broken, shattered. Laying in shards around me, glittering reminders that he's every bit as dangerous as he warned me.

"How could you?" There's less anger in my voice than I want. More pain.

"Because it was true," he snaps. "My father would have broken their neck without a thought. And I would have known that I could've prevented it. If only I was harder with them."

It was his way of protecting them. No wonder he was so harsh with me.

"Why did you leave?"

"I left to make my own money, my own fucking way. And no one can tell me who to threaten. Maybe a good man would have stopped hurting people completely, but not me."

"You did it on your own terms," I say sadly, understanding him with futile sorrow. That's why he had to go after my father. It's why he had to come after me. The one thing he wants more than anything in the world—not money, not things. The ability to choose who he hurts.

I pick up a pawn from the rug. Offer it to him.

He accepts with a solemn expression. "The person who bought your house? Jonathan Scott. That was when I realized the connection. I confronted him, and he admitted the truth."

"He bought it in memory of her?"

"Or to prove something."

"To prove what?"

"That she was right all along, that something sinister was happening in that house."

I move to the carpet, picking up the chess piece. Placing them in haphazard groups on the side table, needing to do something with my hands. The wood is smooth and cool, emotion-less. That's how I wish I could be right now. Instead I'm a wildfire of fear and hope.

Then all the pieces are back on the table. Except the dark wood king, rolled far away.

"How can he prove it?" I ask.

Gabriel looks reluctant to answer. He puts his elbow on his knee, staring at the king. "If I tell you, you have to promise not to go to the house."

My eyes widen. The same thing that Nina told me. Why do they think I'll go there? Something must be happening—there. At the house. I stand and cross the room, hand-scraped wood cold against my feet, and pick up the last piece.

I stand in front of Gabriel, offering. "Don't protect me, shield me. As if I can't handle it. As if I can't fight too. Lead me into battle, and I'll follow you."

Fighting beside him—that's the ultimate victory for me. Not helplessness.

After a moment he takes the king from me. "He's holding a ball. Everyone in Tanglewood society is involved. He believes the person responsible for her death will come."

"My father can't even get out of bed."

Gabriel meets my eyes. "Then he won't be

there."

But I can hear from his voice that he doesn't believe that. "Even if he could get up, why would he attend a ball? When it would prove his guilt to Jonathan Scott?"

A grim smile. "To face your mother's lover? In the house he built for her?"

"Pride," I say, bitter and resigned.

"No, little virgin. Love. It makes men do terrible things."

"Like taking me to the ball?" I ask softly.

"Terrible things," he murmurs his agreement. "Like risk his queen."

CHAPTER THIRTY-ONE

I HELPED THROW a hundred balls in the house, the hostess on behalf of my father. We had party planners and caterers, florists and valets, but I was the one who welcomed guests to our home. I always loved seeing the house lit by chandeliers, sparkling and brimming with champagne. It made me feel closer to my mother, knowing she would have done the same thing if she had been alive.

Except I know she left. She wore a beautiful dress and glittering rubies so that she could leave us behind. Even if she was afraid of my father, why would she leave me?

Now I arrive on the other side, in a dark limo gliding down the long drive. Someone has done extensive work on the house, trimming the bushes and restoring the front. No sign that it was vandalized only a week before. Yellow light glows from the windows, reflected in Gabriel's cold regard.

"We don't have to go in," Gabriel says softly.

He doesn't want us to be here when the truth is revealed. Because he thinks it will protect me? I'm already shattered in a thousand pieces, knowing that I was left behind. Unprotected.

A pawn in my own family.

The tinted window reflects my face back to me—the dark lips and upswept hair, rubies shining around my neck. "Whoever did this has been tormenting me for years, before I even knew he existed. I need to know, Gabriel."

It's with my chin held high, my hand wrapped around Gabriel's arm, that I enter my house for the last time. There's no hostess to greet us, but the house is packed. People spill out from every room. Most of the furniture is still gone, but large rugs and credenzas make the space feel intentional. Men in tuxedos hold silver platters piled with caviar on little spoons.

We continue to the ballroom, where the walls have been redone in a deep gold damask.

A string quartet plays near the parquet floor, a few couples dancing. Behind them is the largest fireplace in the house, almost as tall as a person, flames dancing along with the people. My mother had loved that it warded away the chill in the huge room.

I recognize many faces. Most have been to the

house before. Do they know why they're here tonight? Judging by the way everyone glances at me and whispers, they probably do know. And many of them have seen the naked pictures.

My cheeks flush.

"They can't touch you," Gabriel says.

"It feels like they can," I whisper. "Like they're looking right through my clothes."

His gaze darkens. "Those pictures aren't you. They're a bloody knife. Fingerprints on a window. Evidence of a crime. And anyone who delights in that can go fuck themselves."

I can't help a small, grateful laugh. "I like fighting at your side."

"Good, because I play to win."

My breath catches. We both know this is the last day, the final night bought and paid for at auction. What will happen after this? It's as much a question as who the culprit is.

From across the room I see Nina Thomas holding court from a chair, Charlotte hovering at her side with a glass of water. Nina doesn't look pleased to see me, her gaze decidedly cold.

Does she think I'm in danger? Or does she not want me to find out the truth?

I don't want to believe that she could have done anything to harm my mother. She loved her, in more ways than just a friend. But as Gabriel pointed out, love could make men do terrible things. Women, too. She might have been jealous that my mother got married.

Uncle Landon is here, looking more determined than when I met him at his office. He exchanges a look with me only briefly before turning back toward a man at the center.

His true rival. Not my father like I'd thought.

Jonathan Scott has the same dark eyes as his son, hair shot through with gray. While Damon has an air of good humor, even when he's doing something dark like auctioning a virgin, his father looks hardened by life. Was he that way when my mother fell in love with him? Or did he become that way after her death?

He speaks to a small group of men, their tones hushed, gazes suspicious. And oh God, Justin is with him. Is that who he's talking to about fundraising in Tanglewood? He glances over at me and Gabriel but doesn't break from his conversation.

"My father isn't here," I say, relieved.

I haven't gone to visit him since I returned to Gabriel's house. Maybe I could have used the remainder of the thirty days as an excuse, but the truth was that I didn't want to see him. Didn't want to hear him say any more criticisms of my mother, didn't want to face him with suspicion in my eyes. I don't think he can be the man who took naked pictures of me—but the possibility alone makes my heart careen in my chest, wild and unhinged.

Gabriel snags a glass of champagne from a passing tray. "The night isn't over yet. Have a drink. It will help your nerves."

"What nerves?" I ask with an uneven laugh.

It's a joke because I must look like the picture of anxiety. Not only to find out who scared my mother, who maybe murdered her, but also to face society for the first time since my auction. Most of the men who attended are here tonight. And everyone else surely knows why I'm with Gabriel Miller tonight.

Of course he looks stunning, the picture of masculine elegance and power. Not a hint of worry surrounds him. His tux conforms to his muscled body, emphasizing the breadth of his chest, the taper at his hips. At least a few of the looks coming our way are appreciative of him.

I take a fortifying sip, the bubbling liquid cool down my throat.

Damon Scott appears at Gabriel's side with a genial smile. "Quite a turnout."

"Your father always had a flair for the dramatic," Gabriel responds drily.

"I come by it honest," Damon says, flashing me a wink. "Avery. You're looking absolutely beautiful. Even more than usual, if you don't mind me saying so. What are you doing with this ugly motherfucker?"

The standoff at the Den sits between the three of us, pulsing with tension. "I told him I was coming tonight no matter what, and he came to protect me."

Damon blinks. "That doesn't sound like the Gabriel I know."

"Maybe you don't know him that well."

A startled laugh. "Well, well," Damon says. "Tonight should be very interesting."

"I thought you'd already know the outcome."

He gives me a carefree grin that belies his words. "Not a clue. Didn't Gabriel tell you? I haven't spoken to my father in thirty years. I'm here as a spectator."

I can only stare after him, because there's no way he's older than forty. Not even close. The last time he spoke to his father, he was only a small child. But he came to this ball, where he might speak to him. Where he might confront him. Oh no, he's more than a spectator. He's a participant, caught in the same web as me. I just don't know how.

Chapter Thirty-Two

GABRIEL TOLD ME the upside to his presence was that people tend to tell the truth. They also tend to be kind, smiling and complimenting my dress despite the glint in their eyes. They don't dare make a cutting remark in front of him, but they whisper as soon as we move on.

My insides feel wobbly, but I force myself to smile. This was my home, my mother's home. She wore grace and confidence until her final moments. That's what I'll do too.

I won't give them the satisfaction of breaking in front of them.

Still it's a relief when Ivan and Candy cross the room to meet us. Ivan looks stern and forbidding in a gray suit. Candy looks like a princess in a pale pink dress that wraps around her breasts and falls in flowing silk. Around her neck is a necklace with a pendant shaped like a key and studded with diamonds. I have some idea of what that key represents in their relationship, and I blush.

Candy smiles, knowing and serene. "Hello, Avery."

"Candy." I put my hands on my cheeks in a vain attempt to cool them. "You look lovely, as always."

She turns to Gabriel, studying him with a critical eye. "The past thirty days have been good to you."

"Beyond measure," he replies in a cordial manner. "Ivan. I'm surprised to see you both here."

The gray-eyed man nods. "It's a little past her bedtime, but I'm occasionally generous."

"Ivan, did you just make a joke?" Candy grins. "I think I'm rubbing off on him. Well, more than I usually do. Which I have to admit is quite often."

I swear my cheeks are about to catch fire. How does Gabriel look so calm, only mildly amused by her innuendo? The couple exudes sexuality. I think I get ten degrees hotter just being near them.

Candy giggles at my expression.

My nose scrunches. "You enjoy embarrassing me, don't you?"

"Very much." She grows serious. "The truth is

I wanted to be here in case you need my support."

I glance at Gabriel. "He won't let anything happen to me."

Candy tucks herself against Ivan. "I know that, but I meant emotional support. Our men can be a little…stiff, if you know what I mean."

Damn it, I'm blushing again.

The corner of Gabriel's mouth tilts up. He runs the back of his hand against my cheek, feeling the heat there. His hand is blessedly cool. "Beautiful," he murmurs.

"Yes," Ivan says, though his agreement is more of a clinical appraisal. "And no longer yours, if I read the calendar correctly."

"We still have tonight," I say, feeling defensive.

Except we all know that tonight isn't for fun. This is a night for turning over rocks, for finding out what's been underneath them all along. Shining light into the dark places of my family. A chess match with all the pieces lined up.

A hush falls over the crowd.

I look at the door, and my breath sucks in. Standing in the tall entryway to the ballroom is a man wearing a suit, his hair combed neatly, leaning heavily on a cane. My father.

"No," I whisper.

How can he even be here? He was in the nursing home, barely able to move. He can't be walking. He can't be *here*. Someone would have had to help him. But why?

My mind swerves away from the implications. He came here to face Jonathan Scott like Gabriel predicted. Out of pride, out of love. Or some darker impulse?

The music continues to play. No one told them our personal tragedy is stealing the show, so the sweet strains filter through a shocked crowd, the band playing on the deck of a sinking Titanic.

He couldn't have killed Mama. He couldn't have—

Geoffrey James studies the crowd with an unreadable expression. I hold on to Gabriel's arm tight enough I must be hurting him, but he doesn't flinch. I'm doing it to keep myself from running to my father, fighting the impulse to help him walk. How is he even doing it?

And without a word he continues past the ballroom, down the hallway.

The room takes a collective breath. I burst through the press of people, going after him. I hear Gabriel call my name, but I can't slow down. By the time I reach the stairs, my father is already at the top. And when I make it to his office, he's sitting in his armchair by the fireplace.

"Daddy, what are you doing here?"

He smiles, though it looks more like a grimace. "You didn't visit me again. If my daughter won't come to me, then I have to come to her. I knew you would come."

This close I can see what coming here has cost him, the sickly white of his skin, the sheen of sweat. He breathes heavily even sitting, still using the cane to hold himself upright.

"You should be in the nursing home."

"The one Gabriel Miller paid for?"

"Who cares who paid for it? You need rest."

"So that I can live another month? Another year? That's not a life. I'm ready to go."

"You don't mean that."

"I should have joined your mother a long time ago."

I look away, wondering if they will really be together in the afterlife. "I don't know what to believe anymore, Daddy."

"You doubt me, Avery. Gabriel Miller has made you doubt me."

"Maybe so, but I think I was blind for too long. I wanted to believe that you and Mama were in love, but you weren't. She was scared."

"That again? She told me she heard the house

talking to her, Avery. I loved her, but there was something wrong with her. And even then I suspected it wasn't a drunk driver that caused her accident. She was running from her own demons."

Gabriel appears at the door. "Convenient that she isn't here to refute that."

My father's eyes snap with temporary vigor. "How dare you speak of my wife."

"Tell me you didn't hurt her," I beg softly, kneeling at his side. His hand feels frail between mine. "If you tell me, I'll believe you."

He looks down at me, almost confused, like he isn't sure who I am. "My good girl." He glances at the small table beside us, the marble chess base built into the wood. "Play one more game with me."

"No, Daddy. I'm not going to play a game as if everything's fine."

Sorrow darkens his eyes. "Then he's well and truly taken you from me, hasn't he?"

I want him trapped in every sense of the word, unable to make another move, but alive and fully aware of his loss. That's what Gabriel said he wanted. It's what he's done. The ultimate victory, but he doesn't look pleased. His features are severe, a sentinel by the door, keeping watch over me.

My knight in dark armor.

A scuff from the hall draws my attention. Nina Thomas stands in the doorway, her gaze accusatory, the matronly rose-gold dress incongruous with the venom in her eyes.

Charlotte hovers behind her, looking worried. "Mom, I don't think—"

"This is what we came for, so that I could look this man in the eye and tell him I know what he did. I knew from the beginning. I warned her about you."

I realize now that I don't need the diary to understand my mother. Don't need the house or the confessions of the people who loved her. Because for all that they wanted her, they didn't know her.

My father laughs, breath uneven. "Of course you did."

She moves into the room, leaning on her daughter's arm. "What does that mean?"

"It means Helen told me about your adolescent explorations. She told me that you cared for her more than she did for you, how it embarrassed her."

I suck in a breath, shocked by the cruelty in the words—because there's a ring of truth in them. And judging by the pain in Nina's eyes, she heard it. "I don't believe anything you say," she says fiercely. "You terrorized her. And when she tried to run away from you, you killed her."

My father narrows his eyes. "Or maybe you were angry that she wouldn't leave with you."

My mother was Helen of Troy in every sense, the threat of female power, the destructive beauty of the female form. I know because I walk the same path. Every girl who's lusted after and then blamed for that lust, every woman who's seduced and then accused of liking it.

Stolen and then wrestled back. We're all the epicenter of our own wars.

"More likely you were angry that she left with anyone," Uncle Landon says from the doorway. "I admit it wounded me that she never looked at me as anything more than an amusement, one of her admiring coterie. But I would have helped her if she came to me. That's what pains me the most. That she trusted the wrong person."

The city will define me in its own image—with all the glory and the humiliation of the virginity auction. They don't know me, either. Only Gabriel knows the heart of me, those golden eyes unnerving because they actually see.

And that knowledge gives me the strength to

stand up. "Trusting the wrong person?" I say to Uncle Landon. "That's rich coming from you. My mother trusted you enough to make you the administrator of her trust. And you gambled it away, losing her house."

Tears brighten his eyes. "I know. I'm sorry, Helen."

A shiver runs through me, because it's like he sees her standing where I am.

Am I fated to follow her footsteps to the end?

"And you," I say, turning to Nina. "So determined to make your love affair more than it was. I know how painful it is to love a person who doesn't return it, but that doesn't give you any special right to them. She made her choice."

Nina closes her eyes against my words, shaking her head. A moan of grief escapes her. It turns into a cough that forces her to sit in the nearest chair with her daughter's help.

Charlotte shoots me a worried look. "I need to get her home."

I swallow hard, turning to face my father. "And whatever happened the night she died, you had already failed her. She told you she was afraid, and what did you do? Dismiss her. Deny her."

"She was crazy. What would you have had me do?"

"Believe her. That's what." I shake my head, desperate to make him understand. Because there's only one way someone got those pictures of me—close-ups of my face and body, times when I was naked and unaware. Even sleeping.

I pick up a paperweight made of stone, the shape of a king piece. I gave it to my father for his birthday a few years ago. With a wild swing it slams into the wall. Plaster sprays from the blow, exposing deeper layers of white and the hint of a shadowy space.

Another swing, and more of the plaster falls away. Dust falls around me like rain.

"Christ," Gabriel says, deftly taking the king from me.

"She heard it talking to her," I tell him, out of breath. "The house."

Understanding lights his eyes. Whatever demons chased my mother, they were real. Even fifteen years ago they had plenty of audio devices that could be hidden. And more importantly they had secret cameras. The kind of cameras that could capture me in private moments.

Gabriel glances at the statue as if judging its weight, its strength. And then he smashes it into the wall, making more of a dent than I could. I take a step back, making room, blocking the spray of plaster from hitting Daddy. He failed my mother, but he was still my father.

Damon Scott strolls into the room, expression only mildly curious. "Is this some kind of renovation reality show? Because our ratings will be amazing."

Gabriel sends him a dark look. "Are you going to make jokes or are you going to help?"

Damon opens his mouth, surely to answer with the former, but then seems to think better of it. He joins Gabriel as they pull away more of the wall with their hands.

A black cord appears, something rubbery in Gabriel's hands. He pulls on it, and I realize it's a wire. He yanks hard, dragging a seam through the middle of the wall. The house is coming apart, torn piece by piece by the man I trusted to hold it together. I can't fault him, though. A puzzle needs to be solved. A game needs to be played.

A house of cards needs to come crashing down.

And then the cord snaps taut, unable to release any more. Damon does the honors, pulling something black and square from the wall. A speaker? A camera? Maybe both.

"Fuck," Gabriel mutters, digging away more Sheetrock. The darkness goes too deep. No corresponding wall on the other side, at least not for a while, past the triangle of light from this room. Why is there so much space?

I take a step closer, horror weighing me down. There's a room here. A small room. On the floor I can see more wires. It might be innocuous space, a quirk of old house design, except for the stool sitting inside, old food wrappers piled in a corner. And on the other side of the wall... My mind flinches away from the realization.

That's my bedroom.

Chapter Thirty-Three

S OMEONE MOVES PAST me. My father hobbles closer, an expression of deep fury on his face. "What the hell is that?"

I can't doubt the sincerity of his outrage, but it doesn't help to know my father wasn't involved. Someone had a front-row seat to my room— when I believed I was alone, when I changed my clothes. When I touched myself in bed at night.

This is what my mother sensed, the darkness closing in around her.

And now it's around me, strangling me where I stand. My stomach flips over, the champagne roiling like lava inside. Daddy leans against the wall, staring into the gaping hole.

"She was telling the truth," he whispers, regret ripping through his voice.

Then it's too much to hold back. I turn to the marble fireplace, wretching. I haven't eaten enough to fully vomit, but that only makes it worse, my stomach heaving against nothing.

"Who did this?" The question is quiet, but the entire room turns toward the authority in Gabriel's tone. There's no doubt that the guilty party will suffer under his hand. His glittering gaze scans the room, falling from my father to Nina Thomas to Uncle Landon.

They stare back at him, a mix of guilt and condemnation.

"All of them loved my mother," I say, falling against the cool stone, pressing my cheek to it.

Gabriel shakes his head slowly. "All of them failed her."

Instead I hear in his voice, *all of them failed you*. And the way he looks at me, his jaw tight, his body thrumming with barely leashed violence, he thinks he failed me, too.

"It might not be someone in this room," Damon says, dark with meaning.

My father trembling with the effort to remain upright, even with the cane to lean on. Nina, eyes filled with tears. Uncle Landon, inexpressible sorrow.

I shake my head. "Who else could it be?"

Damon says nothing, his expression as hostile as I've ever seen him. Gone is the good humor that accompanies his every sly request, the cheerfulness that infused even his most serious demand. This is the dark side of him, the one that makes him feared in the city.

"These people might have loved her," Gabriel says. "But she loved someone else."

"Jonathan Scott," I say, gasping.

And that's the fatal flaw in my deductions, the missing piece of logic from my strategy, an overlooked piece in my chess set. So many people loved my mother. And when she finally fell in love, I thought it would be reciprocated. Except what if it wasn't? What if she fell in love with someone who had dangerous intent?

Someone willing to play games with her mind—with her life?

Nina coughs, shaking her large frame. The sound tears at my insides. It's hard to believe she can make that and not rip apart her lungs.

Uncle Landon tilts his head, expression bemused. "Do you smell that?"

I close my eyes with chagrin. "I kind of threw up."

He shakes his head. "Not that, dear girl. It smells almost like—"

"Smoke," I say, voice high with panic.

The sound of shouts drifts upstairs, along with panicked shrieks and feminine screams.

"Get everyone out of the house," Gabriel says

to Damon, who nods.

Damon looks around before narrowing his gaze on Uncle Landon. "You. You're going to help me clear this place. If even one person burns, you're going to pay, understand?"

Uncle Landon looks affronted. "I didn't start the fire."

"I don't care," Damon says, leaving the room with a determined stride. After a brief, panicked look at my father, Uncle Landon follows him quickly, apparently taking the threat seriously.

Between the two of them I hope that they can get the downstairs empty. Uncle Landon knows the layout of the place as well as anyone, and Damon Scott has an authority that won't be questioned.

My father stumbles, a hoarse cry of grief coming from him. I run to his side. Even with the weight he's been losing, it's more than I can support on my own.

"Help me," I beg Gabriel.

He glances at Charlotte. "Can you take care of your mother?"

Nina coughs, struggling to speak. My legs shake under the weight of my father, ready to crumple.

Charlotte waves us away, looking calm and

composed except for the glint of worry in her dark eyes. "Take care of him. I can help her downstairs."

Gabriel pauses, clearly torn. In the end he gives me a terse nod. "Let's go."

We make our way downstairs, navigating the stairs with stark efficiency as the heavy smoke increases around us. My father begins coughing, and I realize Nina's cough will only get worse. Charlotte said she could get her downstairs, but she isn't used to dealing with smoke.

I glance back, but the landing is still empty. Where are they?

"I'll go back for them," Gabriel says, following my line of worry.

Fear nips at my ankles as we hobble outside, struggling to carry my father through the heavy flow of panicked people in tuxes and gowns. Discordant strains of music rise over the sounds of hysteria. The harsh whir and crank of strings in distress. The musicians running for their lives? The instruments trampled in the rush? It matches the frantic melody of our escape.

With a low growl, Gabriel hauls my father over his shoulder and carries him from the house. I trail after them, worried that the position will hurt my father worse. It's with surprising carefulness that Gabriel deposits Daddy on the grass a few yards from the house.

"Stay with him," he orders before disappearing into the house again.

I check on my father, who's coughing even more, unable to speak. After a moment flames leak out of the roof, breaking through the high shingles. Smoke pours out of the top as if the house expels a deep breath. The flow of people out the door slows to a trickle.

Uncle Landon bursts from the house, helping a white-haired woman to the grass, before joining us. "I think we got everyone."

Damon appears, looking haggard. "Where is he?"

"Gabriel?"

"My father."

The sea of people mill around the lawn, looking frightened, pale with shock. A few are clearly excited, their cell phones out to snap pictures and post them online. This is the most excitement Tanglewood society has seen in years. "I haven't seen him."

Damon curses under his breath before charging into the crowd, clearly determined. Except that I know everyone isn't out. Nina Thomas and her daughter aren't anywhere to be seen.

I turn to Uncle Landon. "Gabriel is still upstairs."

He shrugs. "He's stronger than me. If he can't get down, then I can't help him."

Fury washes through me. "Fine."

Then I'm back through the door, Uncle Landon's shout of protest trailing after me.

I make it halfway up the stairs before I pass Charlotte. Nina leans against the wall, almost falling down the stairs while Charlotte tries to support her.

"She's having some kind of attack," Charlotte says, fighting tears.

I help them down the last few steps. "Where's Gabriel?"

"He came back for her, but the fire moved so fast. Maybe it was the open walls, I don't know. But the ceiling started coming down on us. He pushed Mom out into the hallway before a flame blew through the room."

My heart stops. "Oh my God."

Any trace of the cool, calm businesswomen has been replaced by a heartbroken girl. "I tried to get him out, but he yelled at me to go. I'm so sorry."

I take the steps two at a time, faster than I've ever moved through the house. I see what

Charlotte meant, the cascade of flames that have consumed the wall. Is he already dead inside? Already burned?

"Gabriel," I shout.

I don't hear anything, but there's not a chance in hell I'm leaving him here. With a deep breath, as if I'm about to plunge into dark water, I jump over the flames—praying that the floor isn't weak enough to send me crashing down to the first floor. I stumble and fall, a large gash on my forearm making me cry out.

And then I see him. Gabriel, held down by a beam across his chest, fighting to push it off.

His eyes widen. "What the fuck are you doing here?"

"Saving you."

"Get out of here, Avery. Right now."

"I'm not leaving without you." But the beam is too heavy for me to lift—clearly, because he would have been able to remove it himself. "On the count of three."

Even though he looks furious with me, he says, "Three."

I force all my weight into it, all the grief and rage and love I have for Gabriel. He struggles too, his breath coming harder as the beam pushes down on him. Are his ribs broken? My arms quiver with the force I'm using, but the beam barely budges.

Smoke swirls around us, filling my lungs. I cough, shoving uselessly against the beam.

Gabriel manages to grasp my arm. "Avery, listen to me. It's too late. Go outside. Wait for the fire department."

I shake my head, eyes stinging with smoke and tears. There hadn't been any sirens outside. "After the looks we got at the courthouse from the cops? With my family's reputation in this city? I don't think they'll be rushing to my address anytime soon."

"I don't give a fuck," Gabriel says furiously. "You need to go."

And like the fire brought down the walls around us, like the marble chess piece smashed into the Sheetrock, I can see right through to the heart of him. To his doubt and his power. His love, the kind that makes him do terrible things.

"I'm not leaving you."

He must see the determination in my eyes because something like panic crosses his. "You once told me that if I care about you at all, to tell you the truth. And I did, Avery. I did it, even knowing it would bring us here. It would endanger you."

My heart clenches. "Yes."

"And now I need something from you. If you care about me at all, leave. Now."

I kneel at his side, placing a kiss on his cheek. "I care about you, Gabriel. And that's why I can't leave you here."

Then I pick up the small table, knocking the chess pieces to the ground. I shove the circular edge under the end of the beam, creating a lever. The wood in the table cracks but the marble chess base holds steady, lifting the wide beam by an inch.

Gabriel grunts, his expression impassive, but I know the pain must be intense. It will only hurt him worse as I push the beam farther. It's the only way to save him.

Using the carved base of the table, I deepen the angle beneath the beam. I push down with all my strength, able to use my weight pressing down on the lever. The beam shifts with a creak while Gabriel swears profusely, sweat slicking his skin.

The beam slants more sideways, but Gabriel looks deathly white, unable to slide the rest of the way out. And even if he were able to move to the side, the beam would follow him down to the floor.

A pop from above is the only warning before

the ceiling rains down on us. I throw myself over Gabriel's face, shielding him.

"It's too heavy," he says, teeth gritted. "Go. Now."

My mother risked everything for a man who played her. I should be wary of sacrifice by now, but this is one I have to make. "No."

"Avery," he says, words coming sharper, shorter. He can't breathe well. "If you don't leave now, I'll never forgive you. I swear to God, I'll never speak to you again."

"But you'll be alive," I say, moving beneath the beam's end. It's higher now, after the table did its work. "Isn't that what you told me? The ultimate victory? I'm not going to let you be the martyr, Gabriel."

It isn't martyrdom I'm worried about and we both know it. It's him—Gabriel Miller in all his wild, fierce glory. Maybe my mother and I are fated to fall in love with dangerous men. I just hope that mine won't destroy me, too.

I shove against the beam with all my might, panting at the effort.

Someone appears at the door, cursing at the lick of flames. Justin.

Gabriel speaks through obvious pain, the evenness of his voice forced. "Get. Her. Out."

"I'm not leaving until he does," I tell him. "So you might as well help me."

Justin glances from Gabriel to me, his expression solemn. Then he jumps into action, pushing off his suit jacket and joining me beneath the beam. Together we manage to force it higher, maybe an inch, enough for Gabriel to draw in a rough breath.

With a pained shout, Gabriel heaves himself back. His legs just clear the space before my knees give out. Justin swears and drops the beam. With a crack, the other end falls through the floor, revealing a small peek at the ballroom beneath us.

Gabriel closes his eyes, clearly fighting whatever's happening inside him.

I hurry to his side, helping him stand up, finding more strength somewhere inside me. We do what we have to. With his hard-packed muscle and large frame he's much heavier than my father. Justin joins him on the other side, helping to support him. And with struggling, halting steps, we make our way across cracked wood and down broken stairs.

CHAPTER THIRTY-FOUR

WHILE I'M WAITING for the doctor, someone knocks on the door. I look through the peephole, thinking maybe it will be Damon. Or maybe the cops. Instead I recognize Will from the Rose and Crown Motel. He looks out of place with the lush green and wooded stretch behind him, so different from the concrete forest I know him from.

I open the door. "I can't believe you were spying on me."

Even though I can believe it. I know how persuasive Gabriel can be.

Guilt forces his gaze to the side. "I'm sorry."

I move back to let him in. "I just hope you charged him enough."

He steps into the hallway gingerly, as if expecting to be tossed back out. "He didn't pay me anything, I swear."

"Well, then you definitely didn't charge him enough."

"I asked for something more important than money."

"What?"

Is that a blush? His cheeks look a shade darker.

"Come on," I say, wheedling him. "You betrayed me to get this thing that's better than money. The least you can do is tell me."

He's silent a moment. "Fine, I'll tell you. But you can't tell anyone. It's a matter of national security."

"National security?" I say doubtfully.

He nods. "I served in Afghanistan. A guy in my division. God, I hated his guts. Despised him. Wouldn't have seen him while we were on leave, but we both went to this wedding for another teammate. And I met his wife."

My mouth opens on a silent O.

"Got to talking to her. Felt bad that she was married to such a jackass. Everyone knew he was a douche, but even I didn't think he would sleep with one of the bridesmaids. He snuck off and left his wife at the reception. She was embarrassed but not surprised. So I stayed with her. Nothing happened," he adds like that's important.

"It would be better if something had," I say, meaning it. "He didn't deserve her loyalty."

"He didn't," Will says. "But she had kids at home. Two girls. Twins."

"Oh, Will."

"Then the fucker went and got himself blown up. That probably would have been the best case for her, honestly. Except it came out that he wasn't supposed to be in that supply store, that he'd been selling supplies and weapons to the locals."

"Oh shit."

"It shouldn't have mattered to Karen. She should have still gotten full survivor benefits. Without the ability to adjudicate his case while he was alive, he would be considered to have died honorably—no matter what was uncovered after."

"But?"

"But he slept with the major general's wife. So the guy made sure he wasn't just tried for dishonorable conduct, like would usually happen, but treason. There's no statute of limitations on treason. He was found guilty—because he was—and there are special rules for espionage and treason."

"So she didn't get his benefits?"

"Even with two little girls at home, after living on base and moving around for years, living the army life, they got kicked out with nothing. No family either."

My heart sinks. "So what did you ask for?"

"For him to be reinstated. The case will be reviewed by a board and overturned. Technically he's guilty, but it never should have gotten that high. They shouldn't suffer for his mistakes."

"So she'll get full benefits and you'll still be sleeping outside of a shitty motel?"

"Doesn't matter what happens to me."

"It does matter. If you had asked for money, you could have gone to her, been with her."

"And what? Pay her to be with me? Force her to do what's best for her kids? I'd never do that to her." He shakes his head. "Besides, the stain of treason would follow her everywhere. Her girls, too. It's better this way."

"You can still go to her. Now. She'll have the benefits, whether she wants you or not, so she won't feel obligated. You can be together."

A short laugh. "I don't know whether she was even interested in me. And like you said, I'm sleeping outside of a shitty motel. Not exactly good boyfriend material."

"Is she here in Tanglewood?"

He nods.

My eyes narrow. "That's why you're here, isn't it?"

"Leave it alone, Avery. It's done. She's getting what she deserves, and I'm getting what I deserve."

"And what do you deserve?"

"To be alone." His nod has finality. "I only need to confirm it's done with Miller."

I press my lips together, unable to say good-bye.

He hesitates. "Are you…?"

He wants to know if I'm okay. Whether he hurt one woman to save another. "I'm good here."

I set out to save my mother's house, because I thought it was her legacy. Something she passed down to me in a final motherly act. It was a myth I believed because I needed it, the allure a burning desire for love, the threat a cold realization that love wouldn't be enough.

In the end I'm left not with a house or a diary, not with any assurance of my mother's love. Instead I have only what's in front of me—the opposite of myth. I have truth.

CHAPTER THIRTY-FIVE

A S MANSIONS GO Gabriel's home is understated. It doesn't have a bowling alley, a skating rink, or an Olympic-sized swimming pool. No solid-gold molding. The elite of Tanglewood want more pomp and circumstance for their millions.

Instead the house has an unassuming front, two white columns the only adornment. Inside it's spacious but dimly lit, giving the appearance of being cozy.

The library is dark, only embers in the fireplace. I cross the rug to where Gabriel reclines in one of the wide leather armchairs beside the chess set, his posture innocuously casual. You might not guess that he had bruised three ribs and punctured a lung in the house.

He refused a hospital, choosing instead to be seen by his personal doctor. A doctor who had warned me that our patient was particularly stubborn. *Watch for shortness of breath, muscle weakness, fatigue. He probably won't tell you when he gets tired, but he needs to rest.*

He looks the opposite of tired, lounging with leashed power.

"Gabriel. Can I get you something?"

His eyes burn with accusation. "What did you have in mind?"

"Tea. A blanket." I had known he would be angry, but I refuse to let him push me away. "It's only fair that I help you heal."

"If you think this is going to make me go easy on you, think again."

"I know you're mad about the fire," I begin. "You told me not to go to the house."

He leans forward, the slow movement his only concession to injury. "I'm not mad that there was a fire, Avery. At least I'm not mad at you. When we find Jonathan Scott, he'll pay for that."

"Damon hasn't found him yet?"

The last I saw of Damon was at the fire. He's been a man on a mission ever since. After decades of living in the same city, never speaking, Damon wants to kill his father.

"He's gone underground. And when a man like Jonathan Scott goes underground in this city, he's untraceable. A fucking ghost in the twisted machine that is Tanglewood."

"For good?"

"I'm sure he'll strike when we least expect it."

My stomach twists with unease. "And the house?"

"It's coming down." He gives me a sideways look. "Unless you want me to rebuild it."

I swallow hard. "You would do that for me?"

"Haven't you figured that out, little virgin? I would do anything for you."

My heart expands, beating wildly. "Why?"

"Don't change the subject," he says, his voice silky with menace. "All I can think about is spanking your hide until it's pink, and then red, and then black-and-blue. And even then I wouldn't stop punishing you."

"Why?" The word comes out as a squeak.

"I told you to leave."

"Leave you in a burning building?"

"Exactly."

"I could never do that. I mean, I don't even think I could do that for a stranger. And you're—"

"What am I?" he asks, a challenge thick in his voice. "What do you think you know?"

I place my palm against his hard jaw, feel the tension coursing through him. And recognize it for what it is. Fear for me. Love. "I know that you're a man on the edge."

His hand grasps my wrist, squeezing in threat. "On the edge of what?"

"You tell me."

"I would break every single rib over and over again, every goddamn bone in my body if I could stop this horrible feeling, this constant need to have you near me, under me. Wrapped around my cock."

A small laugh escapes. "I think it will be a while before we do that."

Golden eyes narrow. "Why's that?"

My eyes flick down to his chest. A black T-shirt covers him, the thin fabric tracing the lines of his bandages. "You're injured."

"Not too injured for that." He moves my hand down to his jeans. His hard length greets my touch, pulsing against my palm.

"No way. The doctor told me you would be trouble."

A low growl. "I'll show you trouble."

"No, no," I say quickly, knowing he'll make good on his threat. And then he really would hurt himself. "Maybe in a couple weeks we could try something slow—"

"Now."

"But what if you—"

"I'm sure I can think of a way to fuck you

without killing myself." He considers that. "Almost sure. Doesn't matter. There's no way I'm waiting two weeks to feel your sweet cunt."

The word is a stroke between my legs, making me whimper. "It's too soon."

"If you don't climb on top of me, it will be too late."

My eyes widen as I realize he's telling the truth. His erection presses against his pants, taut and large. Just from talking to me, looking at me. He would rather break his bones than need me, but he doesn't get that choice. I thought I was powerless, but he's the one bound.

Carefully, slowly, I climb onto the armchair, placing my knees on either side of his legs. He makes a low sound when I brush against his chest, but when I try to pull away, he clasps me tight.

I reach between us, unleashing his cock. It falls against my stomach, heavy and slick at the tip. I bite my lip, pressing it between my legs. When I look up at him, he's watching the place where we touch, his lids low, hands holding my thighs hard enough to leave marks.

"Dying?" I ask him softly.

He laughs and then groans. "Fuck yes."

I press down, sheathing him, savoring the ache from his size. When I'm seated against him, I can feel his legs under my ass, his coarse hair against my bare skin. He flexes inside me, and my body clenches in response. It's a wordless communion, an echo of the look we share. It's unbearably intimate to see his expression, his need. Unbearably vulnerable to know he sees the same in me.

Rising up, I gasp at the slide of him. When I'm at the apex, his fingertips dig into my hips, dragging me back down again. Our bodies clasp together, and he groans.

"Again," he demands.

My legs tremble, but I obey him, thrusting myself on top of him, using my whole body to pleasure him, shaking muscles squeezing him inside, slick flesh adding friction.

A tortured sound fills the space, and I realize it's me. It's one thing to let him plunder me, to open my legs and feel him slide inside—another thing to be the force of my own submission, to let gravity and my own desire to please him stretch me wide.

It felt like fucking heaven to break you open. That's what he said, and I see that it's true. A strange release to feel the pain, to inflict it, to choose who to hurt. And then his eyes flash with agony, his cock pulses inside me, and his body goes tense as he comes with a loud groan.

My flesh can only ripple around him, only want and need and flux, until his thumb goes to my clit, a rough flick—that's all I need. It sends me over until I'm pressing myself against his hips, my flesh tender against the coarseness of his hair, sex damp with his spend.

I fix our clothes and move to stand. He pulls me back to his lap.

"Look at me," he says, voice soft with threat.

It's a struggle, but I meet his gaze. "Gabriel."

"I thought you were going to die in that house."

"We're safe now," I whisper, wanting to reassure him. Wanting to reassure myself.

But I'm not sure we can ever be safe with Jonathan Scott in the city. He killed my mother. I know that now. That house was my family's castle. We were invaded by a Trojan horse in the form of hidden cameras, ripped apart by a weapon in the form of a secret.

And Jonathan Scott could strike again at any time.

For now we're safe behind thick walls.

We need to fortify them for whatever comes next.

"I thought I was going to have to *watch* you

die, Avery. Do you know what that did to me? Seeing you in danger and unable to help you?"

The anguish in his eyes rips a hole through my shield. I have nothing to protect me, nothing to do but admit the truth. "It would have done the same thing to me if I'd left you there."

I touch my forehead against his, closing my eyes. He pulls in a shuddering breath.

"Then we both lost," he murmurs. "A stalemate."

"Both of us helpless. Both of us trapped." The fate he wanted for my father, but it bound us together instead. A curse reflected in black-and-white, each side a mirror.

Neither of us can escape. Neither of us wants to.

"To remain," he says, his hands tightening on mine.

And that's what we are. I wouldn't change it for the world. Not for a million dollars. Some games you prefer to lose. I will remain on this board with him, the man I love.

"Play with me?" I whisper against his lips.

"Always."

EPILOGUE

W E SPEND THE next week in bed, in the library. In his office. Doing all manner of illicit things, some even illegal in a few states. Neither of us feel inclined to leave the safety of these walls. But eventually the world intrudes. Gabriel gets a call from Charlotte telling him a merger needs his attention.

He's dressed in a suit, his jaw freshly shaved, his eyes veiled. Standing in the middle of the room, he exudes confidence and strength. I wouldn't want to be on the other side of the chessboard to him like this.

I leave the bed, my nightgown a slinky contrast to his stark power. "Have a nice day, Mr. Miller."

He tucks me against his side, the suit fabric cool against my arms. "Are you sure you'll be okay?"

"Of course." I give him a chiding look. "You're the one healing from fractured ribs. I'm

278

completely fine."

That's not entirely true. I suffered some smoke inhalation during the fire. Wracking coughs that went on for days. Or maybe just minutes. And worse than the cough are the nightmares. Flames. Fear.

Gabriel's expression darkens. "I'll stay home."

And every night Gabriel has been there to wake me up, to hold me in his arms, to murmur reassurance. At one time I wouldn't have believed he could be tender. Now I know what's underneath the muscle and flesh, the sternness and dark sensuality.

"Hey," I tell him softly. "You're only a phone call away. And you'll be back tonight."

He frowns. "A half day."

My heart does a jump with relief. The truth is I want him to come home quickly. I don't want him to leave at all. But I don't want him to worry about me. If I don't convince him I'm okay he'll stay out of obligation. "Take as long as you need. Trust me, I need a long soak in that tub of yours with all the spray jets. Actually it will be good for me. I'm a little…sore."

He narrows his eyes. "Are you trying to get rid of me?"

"Is it working?"

"No."

I smile. "Good. Because I want you home. Once I'm well rested we can spend all night getting reacquainted. Ten hours is a long time to go without seeing you."

"Oh, little virgin. Ten hours? After two you'll be all closed up again, your body tight and fully healed. It will be my pleasure to tear you apart again."

Heat sparks in my core, spreading along my skin like wildfire. My cheeks heat. "Maybe you could be a little late?"

He smiles coolly, enjoying my discomfort. "I couldn't possibly. I'm sure you'll be fine."

I press against his side, savoring the hardness of him. "Are you sure?"

"Don't go anywhere," he warns, ignoring my plea. "If you need something talk to Blue."

Security has been outrageous here ever since the fire. Patrols as if we're in some kind of military compound. Men at every exit. More cameras installed. It's supposed to make me feel safe, but I can't shake the nervous anticipation.

"I'll stay here," I promise.

With a single hard press of his lips against mine, he's gone.

After a few minutes of aimless wandering in

his room, I head into the bathroom. The tub is truly lovely, large and filled with jets, water pouring down from a ledge built with stone. Little glass pots on the side are filled with everything I could want, and I pour in a small scoop of sea salt and a few drops of lavender oil. Steam fills the room, coating every shiny and reflective surface. It's like bathing in a cloud. I close my eyes, breathing in the relaxing aroma.

The doorbell chimes. I jolt with surprise, sending water over the ledge.

My breathing is too fast. *You're safe,* I remind myself.

There's more protection here than at Tanglewood City Hall. Not to mention, if anyone had bad intentions they probably wouldn't announce themselves by using the doorbell.

I grab a thick white towel and step out of the bathtub, taking care on the slippery floor. I dress in jeans and a T-shirt, my wet hair in a ponytail.

A man named Blue is in charge of security here. Apparently he owns a prestigious company that does protection for businesses, even celebrities. Gabriel insisted that he personally oversee my safety.

My heart skips a beat when I see what's leaning against the wall.

Large and flat, wrapped in brown cardboard. "That's me," I say. "That's mine."

Even before I look at the label from the antiquities dealer in Maine, I know that it's my mother's portrait. I started looking for it as soon as the escrow account transferred to my name. Gabriel offered to buy it for me, but I refused. It's important that the money from the auction goes toward rebuilding my life. My virginity will always be twisted with shame and responsibility, with darkness and dread, but there's one bright spot. Because with that money comes independence.

I'm here by choice. I'm with Gabriel because I want to be.

It cost a small fortune to track down the picture. The original dealer had sold it to an anonymous buyer. I had to pull a Polaroid from insurance records and send it all over the country. Finally I found it. The agent I spoke with over the phone assured me it was the same painting. He even sent me a digital picture from his phone to confirm. I bought it from him immediately and had it shipped.

Blue's expression is usually intimidating, military presence combined with hard experience. Now it turns even more forbidding. "I need to inspect the package, Ms. James."

"I appreciate you taking the job seriously, but it's just a painting. And it's kind of personal."

He nods without apparent sympathy. "I need to inspect it first."

I hold back a sigh. "Okay."

"If you could wait upstairs." From the look on his face, this isn't a request. It's an order. And I'm guessing this man isn't used to being disobeyed.

I know he's under the strictest orders from Gabriel, so I take pity on him. "You have five minutes."

Once upstairs I linger on the landing, elbows resting on the balcony. Blue glances at me, and I know he wants to tell me to go away. What does he think is in that package—a bomb?

He must think better of it, because he pulls out a pocket knife and slits the cardboard. I cringe, not wanting the blade to touch the painting, but there's some padding underneath. And Blue is very careful, I'll give him that. Even from far away I can see his delicate handling of the piece.

From here all I can see is jewel tones in the paint, a champagne gold frame.

Excitement twists my stomach into knots. I force myself to stand still as Blue runs his hands along the sides and inspects the backing. If there's even a speck of dust on that painting he'll find it. That's how carefully he covers every inch.

He takes his protection duties seriously, I'll give him that much.

Helen of Troy has been represented in wildly different ways, from a dark seductress to an unwitting spoil of war. Her agency and motivations vary in every depiction, but one fact holds true. She was the most beautiful woman in the world. The ancient Greeks didn't consider beauty to be in the eye of the beholder. It was an objective trait, the universal value of a woman. Helen was the definitive best, all others judged against her perfection.

Every story of my mother is both true and false. Even the one she told herself through her diary. Filled with hopes and desires and dreams. With love for a man who didn't deserve it.

In the end all I have left is her beauty, immortalized in this painting.

Finally Blue stands back and nods to me. "It's clear."

I dash down the curving staircase, eager to see the painting that had once been so familiar to me. I haven't seen it in months, aside from the photographs. They're too dark to see details, too impersonal to feel her presence. Now I get to see the real thing.

Blue has replaced some of the brown packing paper over the painting, maybe in deference to the fact that he opened it. I pull the paper away.

And I'm looking in a mirror.

Not the kind made of glass, not the kind that frosts over in a bath. This is a mirror made of acrylics and canvas, color and shadows. A painting, but it's not my mother. It's me.

She and I look similar, but this painting is different. My eyes are a little wider, a little more innocent. My blonde hair falls around my shoulders instead of pulled up. I'm smiling instead of solemn. And I'm wearing a glittering pink dress I remember from my society days.

It's definitely me.

Right on the canvas where my mother should be. My stomach drops for miles.

Horror. Dread. Anger that someone defiled my mother's painting.

The frame looks the same, so that means they removed the old one and replaced it with this. Or maybe just painted right over, someone with skill and artistry and dark intent.

I look at Blue in shock, expecting to see some kind of reaction from him.

He looks at me with bemusement, unaware that the painting should be something else. He probably noticed it was me right at the beginning, but he assumed that it should be.

"Gabriel," I whisper. *I need you, Gabriel.*

Blue's gaze narrows, flicking to the painting and then back to my expression. Whatever he sees spurs him into action. He gets on the phone. "Get me Miller," he says in curt tones.

Gabriel will come back, but I don't know what he can do. He vanquished my father for stealing from him. Turned away Justin with a terrifying look. Even tore through a burning building. But he can't find Jonathan Scott. He has roots in this city, dark and winding. Even Gabriel can't penetrate them.

Someone killed my mother. And as I stare at my picture, I wonder if I'm next.

THE END

Thank You!

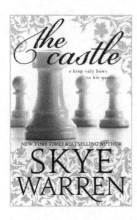

Thank you so much for reading THE KNIGHT!

This book ends with Gabriel and Avery together, but their story doesn't end here. Follow them into THE CASTLE as they face the fight of their lives!

SIGN UP FOR SKYE WARREN'S NEWSLETTER: www.skyewarren.com/newsletter

If you loved The Pawn, you'll love the sensual, dark, and dangerous USA Today bestselling Stripped series. The prequel novella Tough Love is FREE to one-click at all online book retailers! By the way, this is the series where Ivan and Candy first appear.

And don't miss the rough + sexy bestselling

Chicago Underground series, starting with ROUGH! *I never thought a man that rough could be my prince…*

And if you're looking for something sexy and sweet and romantic, you can fall in love with this modern fairy tale retelling! You can find the first part Beauty Touched the Beast, at all retailers now.

I appreciate your help in spreading the word, including telling a friend. Reviews help readers find books! Please leave a review on your favorite book site.

You can also join my Facebook group, Skye Warren's Dark Room, for exclusive giveaways and sneak peeks of future books.

Turn the page for an excerpt from Tough Love…

Excerpt from Tough Love

THE MOON SITS high above the tree line. Somewhere beyond those woods is an electric fence. And beyond that is an entire city of people living and working and *loving* each other. I may as well be on the moon for how close I am to them.

A guard walks by my window at 10:05 p.m. Right on time.

I wait a few minutes until he's out of earshot; then I flip the latch. From there it's quick work to push up the pane with its bulletproof glass. I broke the lock a year ago. And almost every night since then I've sneaked down the ornate metal trellis—like a thief, stealing a moment to myself.

The grass is still damp from the rain, the ground beneath like a sponge, sucking me in. I cross the lawn, heart beating against my chest. I know exactly where the guards are on their rounds. I know exactly where the trip wires are that will set off the alarms. My father is too busy in his office to even glance outside.

The office I broke into this morning.

I breathe a sigh of relief when I reach the pool. I'm still out in the open, but the bright underwater lights make it hard to see anything on the patio. They make it hard to see me as I curve around the edge and reach the pool house.

The door opens before I touch the handle. "Clara," comes the whisper.

I can't help but smile as I slip into the dark. Giovanni always opens the door for me. It's like some old-world chivalry thing, even though we're just two kids sneaking around. At least, that's how everyone treats me. Like a kid. But when I'm with him, I feel less like a girl, more like a woman.

He looks out the door for a beat before shutting and locking it. "Are you sure no one saw you?"

"You're such a worrywart, Gio." I let myself fall onto the couch, facing up.

"If your father ever found out…"

We'd be in so much trouble. My father is a member of the mob. Giovanni's father is a foot soldier who works security on the grounds. Both our dads are seriously dangerous, not to mention a little unhinged. I can't even think about how bad it would be if they caught us sneaking around after dark.

I push those thoughts away. "Did you bring it?"

Reluctantly, Giovanni nods. He gestures to the side table, where a half-full bottle of Jack Daniels gleams in the faint light. "Did you?"

I reach into the pockets of my jeans and pull out two cigars. I hold them up and grin. "Didn't even break a sweat."

He rolls his eyes, but I think he's relieved. "This was a bad idea."

"It was my idea," I remind him, and his cheeks turn dark.

Of course the little homework assignment was my idea. I'm the one ridiculously sheltered up in my room with the tutors and the gilded locks. Fifteen years old and I've never even been out to the movies. Giovanni gets to go to regular school. He's too young to get inducted, but I know he gets to be at some of the sit-ins.

"I just want to try them," I say. "I'm not going to get addicted or anything."

He snorts. "More likely you'll get a hangover. How are you going to explain puking to your padre?"

"Honor will cover for me." My sister always covers for me. She takes the brunt of my father's anger. Ninety-nine percent of the time, I love the way she protects me. But one percent of the time, it feels like a straitjacket. That's why I started coming to the pool house. And I'm glad I did. This is where I met Giovanni.

He examines the cigar, eyes narrowed.

"How do you even light it?" I ask. I've seen my father do it a hundred times, but I'm still not clear on how the whole thing doesn't just catch fire. Isn't it made from dried plants?

He puts the cigar to his lips experimentally. It looks strange seeing his full lips around something I've mostly seen my father use. Then he blows out a breath, miming how it would be. I imagine white smoke curling in front of his tanned skin.

"They don't let you use them when they do?" I ask.

He gives me a dark look. I'm not supposed to talk about the side jobs he does for his father. "I mostly sit in a corner and hope no one notices me. It's boring."

"If it's boring, then why won't you talk about it?" I know it's not a good thing to be noticed by men like our father, to be groomed by them, but sometimes that seems better than being ignored. I'm the younger one. And a girl. And there are rumors that I'm not even my father's legitimate child. In other words, I'm lucky my sister remembers to feed me.

He swears in Italian. "That's no life for you, Clara."

"And it's a life for you?"

"I would leave if I could," he says. "You know that."

"You turn eighteen in a year. Will you leave then?" My stomach clenches at the thought of him gone. I'm two years younger than him. And even when I turn eighteen, I won't be leaving. By then I'll be engaged to whoever my father picks for me.

Just like my sister. I shudder at the thought of her fiancé.

He shrugs. "We'll see."

I roll my eyes. I suspect he's making plans, but he isn't sharing them with me. That's how the men around here operate, keeping girls in the dark. Honor only found out she was engaged when Byron was invited over for dinner. He has the money and the power. She doesn't get a choice. Neither will I.

"If you go, you should take me with you," I say.

"I don't think Honor would appreciate me taking you away."

No, she wouldn't. And the thought of being

without my sister makes my heart ache. Sometimes I give her a hard time, but I love her. I'd never leave her behind. "She can come with us. It will be like an adventure."

"Don't talk stupid, Clara." His eyes flash with anger and something else I can't define.

I jerk back, hurt. "It was just an idea."

"Well, it's a bad idea. Your father is never gonna let you leave."

Deep inside, I turn cold. I know that's true. Of course it is. Giovanni doesn't have the money or the resources to take us away from here. And even if he did, why would he want to?

I hate myself for even suggesting it. How desperate can I look?

Shaking inside, I stand up and grab the bottle of Jack Daniels. It's heavier than I would have expected, but I carry it over to a wet bar still stocked with decanters and wine glasses. No liquor though. There used to be huge parties here. When my mother died, they stopped.

We're supposed to have a party in a few days, though, to celebrate my sister's engagement. I'm not even allowed to go. I'll just be able to see the fireworks from the window.

Without a word Giovanni joins me, his heat both comforting and stark. He takes the glass from my shaking hand. He opens the bottle and pours the deep amber liquid inside. Then takes another cup for himself, twice as full.

"Why do you get more?" I protest, mostly because I like teasing him.

His expression is amused. "I'm bigger than you."

He is bigger. Taller and broader, though still skinny. His hands are bigger than mine too. They hold the glass with confidence, whereas I almost drop mine.

I take a sip before I can second-guess myself. "*Oh my God.*"

It burns my throat, battery acid scalding me all the way down.

His lips firm, like he's trying not to laugh. "Good stuff?"

"Oh, shut up." Then it doesn't matter because I'm laughing too. That stuff is *awful.*

He grins and takes a drink—more like a gulp. And he doesn't cough or wince after. "You get used to it."

"How much do I have to drink to get used to it?"

"More than you should."

I take another sip. It burns again, but I have to say, not as bad. It still doesn't taste good, but

I'm determined to drink it anyway. This pool house is the only place where I can break the rules, where I can experience things. The pool house is the only place I even feel alive.

"Let's try mine," I say. My voice already sounds rougher from the alcohol.

He holds up the cigar. "Did you bring a lighter?"

"Oh, crap."

His eyes crinkle in that way I love. It makes my chest feel full, like there's no room for air. "It doesn't matter," he says.

"But I didn't hold up my end of the bargain."

He takes another drink. It looks so natural when he does it. "What bargain?"

"To do bad things," I say seriously. When your life is as controlled as mine, you need to plan these things. Tonight is supposed to be the night.

He looks down, a strange smile on his face. "Let's start with the whiskey. If that's not enough, we can knock over a bank or something."

I smack his arm. "You're making fun of me."

"Never." His eyes meet mine, and I see that he's not laughing at all. "I'd rob a bank if you wanted me to."

My stomach twists at his solemn tone. "I'd rather you stay safe," I whisper.

He reaches a hand toward me like he's going to cup my face, only half an inch away he freezes. I can almost feel the heat of him, and I remain very still, waiting to see what he'll do next.

He shoves his empty glass onto the bar and walks away.

I let out a breath. What is that about? Lately we keep having these moments where it seems, like he's going to touch me. But he never does. I want to touch him too, but I don't. I wouldn't know where to start. I can't even imagine how he'd feel. Would he be like the whiskey, leaving a trail of fire? I'm scared to find out.

He's on the couch, so I join him there. Not touching, just sitting beside him.

"Gio, I'm worried about Honor."

He doesn't look at me. "She's strong. She can take care of herself."

"Yeah, but Byron is a jerk." And even she can't fight the tides. That's what men like Byron are. Tsunamis. Hurricanes. Natural disasters.

"Your dad wants someone who can take over. That's pretty much guaranteed to be an asshole."

He's not saying anything I don't know, but it's still frustrating. It's too dark to see his expression. I can only see the shape of him beside me, his neck and shoulders limned by moonlight.

"This isn't the eighteenth century. This is Las Vegas."

"Marriage isn't about that. Not here."

It's about making alliances. It's about *money*. "He should make *you* the next one in line."

At least Gio has been around for years. His dad is trusted here, even if he's not high ranking. This Byron guy hasn't even been in Las Vegas very long. And he's a cop. I learned from an early age not to trust cops—even dirty ones.

Gio shakes his head. "No, thanks."

"Why not? You'd be good at it." I can tell he's biting his tongue. "What?"

"Good at killing people?" he asks softly.

I flinch. Most of the time we skirt around what exactly my father does. And technically Gio is a part of that. I've never asked him if he's killed someone. For all I know, he already has robbed a bank. He's still in high school, so they're keeping him light. But once he graduates high school, they'll want to induct him. I'd almost rather he did leave then. Even though it would kill me to see him go.

He shakes his head. "Anyway, if it were me being groomed, I'd have to marry Honor. And I couldn't do that."

The thought of him marrying my sister makes

my stomach knot. He's only a couple years younger than her. It's actually not a bad idea. "Why not?"

"Because I like her sister."

I go very still. There's only one sister. *Me.*

"What did you say?" I whisper.

"You heard me." He leans close. He reaches for me—and this time, his hand does cup my cheek. The feel of him is shocking, startling, impossibly coarse and warm at the same time. He runs his thumb along my skin, rasping against me. My eyes flutter closed.

The old leather of the couch creaks as he leans forward. He must be inches away now. His breath coasts over my lips. Goose bumps rise on my skin. I'm waiting…hoping…

Suddenly his lips are against mine, warm and soft. God, I've seen those lips smile and twist and curse a blue streak, but I never imagined they could be this soft. Nothing like whiskey, with its fire. This is a gentle heat, a caress, and I sink into him, let myself go lax.

One second later, he's gone. Not touching me at all.

My eyes snap open. "Gio?"

He looks tormented. I may not have felt the whiskey burn, but he did. Pain flashes through his eyes. He stands and walks away. "No, Clara. That was wrong. I was wrong to do that."

"But why?" How could that be wrong? That was the best thing that ever happened to me. On a night when I wanted to be *bad,* I experienced my first kiss. It's the best bad thing I could have imagined. And it tasted so sweet.

He's still shaking his head, so vehemently I'm not sure who he's trying to convince—me or himself. "You've been drinking."

"One drink," I say, kind of insulted. I may be new to this, but I'm not drunk.

"One drink is enough."

"You had one drink too," I point out, accusing.

He laughs, the sound unsteady and harsh. "I'm bigger than you."

I don't know if he means the drink affects him less or if it's just another reason why the kiss was a bad idea—as if he might have overpowered me. But there is no reason why this is a bad idea. I've wanted him to kiss me forever. And judging by the way he kissed just now, he liked it too. Unless…

My voice is small. "Did I…do it wrong?"

He lets out a string of curse words. "No, *bella.* You did nothing wrong. This is me. I can't touch you when you've been drinking. I can't touch you at all."

Want to read more? Tough Love is available on Amazon, iBooks, Barnes & Noble, Kobo, and other book retailers!

OTHER BOOKS
BY SKYE WARREN

Stripped series
Tough Love
Love the Way You Lie
Better When It Hurts
Even Better
Pretty When You Cry
Caught for Christmas
Hold You Against Me
To the Ends of the Earth

Chicago Underground series
Rough
Hard
Fierce
Wild
Dirty
Secret
Sweet
Deep

Criminals and Captives series
Prisoner

Standalone Dark Romance
Wanderlust
On the Way Home
His for Christmas
Hear Me
Take the Heat

Dark Nights series
Keep Me Safe
Trust in Me
Don't Let Go

The Beauty series
Beauty Touched the Beast
Beneath the Beauty
Broken Beauty
Beauty Becomes You
The Beauty Series Compilation
Loving the Beauty: A Beauty Epilogue

About the Author

Skye Warren is the New York Times bestselling author of contemporary romance such as the Chicago Underground and Stripped series. Her books have been featured in Jezebel, Buzzfeed, USA Today Happily Ever After, Glamour, and Elle Magazine. She makes her home in Texas with her loving family, two sweet dogs, and one evil cat.

Sign up for Skye's newsletter:
www.skyewarren.com/newsletter

Like Skye Warren on Facebook:
facebook.com/skyewarren

Join Skye Warren's Dark Room reader group:
skyewarren.com/darkroom

Follow Skye Warren on Instagram:
instagram.com/skyewarrenbooks

Visit Skye's website for her current booklist:
www.skyewarren.com

COPYRIGHT

The Knight © 2017 by Skye Warren
Print Edition

Cover design by Book Beautiful
Formatting by BB eBooks

70563787R00190

Made in the USA
San Bernardino, CA
03 March 2018